# The Women and Men Who Love Them

DR. BRENDA DAVIS-WORRLES

Copyright © 2023 by Dr. Brenda Davis-Worrles

ISBN:   978-1-77883-154-6 (Paperback)

All rights reserved. No part of this publication may be reproduced, distributed, or transmitted in any form or by any means, including photocopying, recording, or other electronic or mechanical methods, without the prior written permission of the publisher, except in the case brief quotations embodied in critical reviews and other noncommercial uses permitted by copyright law.

The views expressed in this book are solely those of the author and do not necessarily reflect the views of the publisher, and the publisher hereby disclaims any responsibility for them.

BookSide Press
877-741-8091
www.booksidepress.com
orders@booksidepress.com

# CONTENTS

The RN's Pledge ........................................................................ 1

Chapter One ............................................................................. 1

Pains and Triumphs ............................................................... 18

Chapter One ........................................................................... 41

Chapter Two .......................................................................... 42

Chapter Three ........................................................................ 44

Chapter Four .......................................................................... 45

Chapter Five ........................................................................... 46

Chapter Six ............................................................................. 47

Women Talking About Adventures of their Sex Lives ........ 51

Jennie's Story ......................................................................... 53

Teresa Story ........................................................................... 54

Barbara ................................................................................... 55

The Ups and Downs in Life ................................................. 59

Debbie .................................................................................... 72

Paulette .................................................................................. 85

# The RN's Pledge

## Chapter One

All Pam's life she has had to struggle. Just thinking back to when she was growing up. Pam and her sisters had to do so much around the house. She had five sisters and five brothers. Pam and her sibling had a pack, they would now tell on each other. So their mom told them that she would whip all of their asses until she got the right one. The crazy thing about the mother she would make everyone take a bath before she would whip them. Then she would lined them up in the hall and whip them by their ages. She never got tired; it was as though she has an iron arm. Pam's older sister Paula got tired of her mom making her do all of the work, taking care of her sibling while she ran the street.

They lived in a brick house and the mom thought that the house was too good for Paula to wash the shitty diapers in it. So Paula had to go outside while snow and ice was on the ground to wash her sister's shitty diapers. Paula cried all of the time. Her fingers were frost bitten but her mom just did not care.

Pam told Paula that she was going to go to school and make something out of herself because she did not want to stay around her mom all of her life.

When Paula turned nineteen she ran away from home. No one knew where she was. Pam heard rumors that she was in college and doing great.

Pam was the last to leave home and she was so glad. Pam when to Lane College to become a RN and she graduated at the top of her class. She was so glad to get away from her lowdown mother. Pam prayed that she would never have to go back home. She did keep in touch with the rest of her siblings except of Paula; she just did not know where she was.

After graduating she got hired at Vanderbilt University Hospital and she really enjoyed her job. She began to see a lot of doctors that she liked and she did not care what flavor they were. Pam made a pledge that she was going to get all the penises that she could because you only live once.

Pam started going after Dr. Fox, he was very handsome. Pam saw him walking down the hall and she dropped her pen on to the floor. Dr. Fox bend over to pick it up and she grabbed his nipple and rolled it through her fingers. Dr Fox looked at her and he smiled. Then he whispered in her ear and told her that, it really gave him a hard on and that he wanted to see what she was mad out of.

Pam told him for a fee, she would meet him when they got off of work. Pam gave doctor Fox her phone number. Dr. Fox called her an hour after he got off of work and told her to meet him at the Radissons Hotel in an hour in Room 244.

Pam was so excited. She put on a maid uniform under her trench coat and placed all of goodies in a bag. She entered the room but Dr. Fox was in the shower. Pam waited until he came out and she was lying on the bed with a whip in her hand. Pam told Dr. Fox that he had been a bad boy and to bend over so that she could give him a whipping. Dr. Fox bend over and she gave him two taps on that ass. Dr. Fox told her to hit him a litter harder. Pam hit him and he got hard as a rock. She told him for a white due, you got it going on. Dr. Fox lay down on the bed and Pam got a feather and started going up and down from his penis to his butt hole. Dr. Fox told her that he had never met anyone like her before. Pam placed a condom on his hard member and she started riding him just like a jockey riding a racehorse. Dr. Fox was really enjoying himself.

Pam told him to suck her breasts and he sucked them as though they were chocolate covered strawberries. Then she told him that she wanted to do it doggie style and he complied. They sucked and fucked until 1 am. The both of them were so drained and Pam was walking bow legged. Dr. Fox told her that he really enjoyed himself and that they would have to do this again. Dr. Fox gave Pam an envelope with 5,000 in it. Pam told him that she was just playing with him but thanks for the money. Dr. Fox told her that there was more where that came from as long as this will stay between the both of them because he was a married man. Pam told him that it was fine with her.

Pam and Dr. Fox continued their relationships for two years until Dr. Fox decided to move to New York. Pam was not upset because she had gotten enough money out of the relationship.

Pam did not fool with too many folk; she just liked to be by herself. Pam decided to leave Vanderbilt and apply at East Tennessee Home Health. Pam started off with five patients a day and she really enjoyed working with the elderly patients.

One of her patient was Chinese and the patient had a young son. He was very handsome and Pam started liking him. Jim Lee made sure that he came to visit his mom each day that Pam had to come to see his mom. When Pam finished taking care of Jim's mom, he walked her to the car. He told Pam that she was a very beautiful lady and he had ever dated outside of his race. Pam told him that color did not matter to her. Jim Lee asked her could he take her out and Pam told him that he could but do not let his mom know. So Jim Lee agreed.

Pam and Jim Lee had been dating for three months before she decided to give her some of her kitty cat. He took to the Radisson Inn. Pam never knew about the size of a Chinese penises but she was ready to find out. She put on her new Victoria's Secrets negligee. Jim Lee crawled up on the bed and he told Pam that Chinese man is going to tear that pussy up. Pam told him to bring it on. Each time Pam would cut the light on, Jim Lee would cut it off. This went on until Pam saw the size of this penis. Pam said to herself this is the sorriest penis I ever seen. They start making love. Pam told him to get up and get between her thighs. He told Pam that China man not finished wearing your kitty cat out. Pam told him to get his little dick ass up out of her pussy. China man got mad and tried to hit Pam. Pam kicked the shit out of him and she put on her clothes so quick and she left.

Pam was so glad that Jim Lee did not know where she stayed. The next day she went to her Supervisor and asked her could she give her another patient in place of Mrs. Lee. Her Supervisor agreed with her.

The next day when Pam went into work to get some paper work, Jim Lee was in the office. He wanted to talk to her but Pam refused. He told her that she will pay for kicking him. Pam told him to kiss her black ass. He told her that he would have if she had of stayed a little longer. Pam's Supervisor came out of her office to see what was going on. Pam told her that Mr. Lee is upset because she decided not to work with his mom anymore. Jim Lee got mad and he left.

Pam was a little scared when she went of her car. She kept looking in her rearview mirror to make sure that she was not being followed. She finally finished her cases. Pam went home and got ready for bed because she was tired. She heard a noise, she got her baseball bat and she went down stairs. Out of nowhere she felt pain in her back. She heard Jim Lee say, you thought that I would not fine your black ass but you were wrong. I just had to give your replacement one thousand dollars to give me your address.

Pam began to pray that the LORD would give her strength. Jim Lee tried to fuck her from behind. Pam reached and she got the bat and she came over her head and hit Jim Lee in the top of his head and he fell out. Pam called 9-11, the police came and Jim Lee was still unconscious. The police told her that she was very lucky and that he had been doing this to a lot of women. Jim Lee had a one million dollar reward for his arrest because the police had been looking for him for ten years. Pam was so thankful that the LORD spared her life and was glad to get the reward.

The next day Pam went to work, she saw Lisa. Pam spoke but Lisa did not but she did have a smirk on her face. Pam said, to herself, yea I got you. Lisa loved to go to Starbucks to get the Mocha Latte. Lisa always would place the leftover latte in fridge and then she would go on her visits. The next day Pam came in early and she melted some exlaxs in Lisa's latte. Pam went on to her cases. Three hours later Pam got a call from her Supervisor to say that Lisa had an accident and she had to leave. She asked Pam could she finish out Lisa assignments and that she would pay her double time and Pam agreed. Pam hung up the phone and she laughed out so loud and said, bitch I got you with your shitty ass.

The next day Pam went in but Lisa still had not returned to work and she was asked again to take over Lisa's assignments.

Lisa finally came back to work and she was mad as hell because she just knew that Pam had placed something in her drink. She did not want to go to her supervisor because she did not have proof. Pam had to go to the bathroom before she went out on her cases. Lisa came into bathroom and she told Pam, bitch, I know you place something in my drink and I am going to beat your ass. Pam told her to bring it on. Lisa swung at Pam but Pam ducked and hit Lisa in her stomach. Lisa wind was knocked out of her and she bend over and Pam hit her in the top of her head and she fell to the floor. As Pam was leaving out of the bathroom, the supervisor was coming in. She saw Lisa lying on the floor and she asked Pam what happen. Pam told her that I guess she is still weak from all of that shitting she did over the last three days.

The supervisor went to help Lisa up but she would not get up. So she had to call 9-11. Lisa had to stay in the hospital because she has a concussion.

Their supervisor asked Pam to pick-up some of Lisa's cases for her until she was able to come back to work, so Pam agreed. Pam had 10 patients a day and she did not get home until 5 pm each day and she was so tired. Pam decided that she needed to go out on Saturday night and have some fun.

Pam went Club 192. She was just sitting at the bar and this guy sat by her. He asked her what her name was and she told him. He told her that his name was Tim and he wanted to dance with her. They went out on the dance floor and danced to a slow song. Tim was really a good dancer. He began to dance to close and each time she would move back. He continued to do it and his dick got hard but it did not stretch out that much. Pam said to herself, I am so tired of the little dick as fuckers. Pam just left off of the dance floor. She told the Bartender that she should have stayed at home. Pam said goodbye to the Bartender and she left. Tim followed her to her car. He pulled her on her arm and she jerked it from him. Tim told her that she thought that she was all that and a bag of chips. Pam told him to get the hell out of her face. He told her that, oh you know you want me. Pam told time that she did not like little ass dick men. Tim told her you got me messed up with the others guys that you have dated. Pam told him that his dick was so little and if it took it out it would not touch his car door. Tim turned two shades of black. Pam thought to herself, her I go again. Tim pushed her and she stumbled but caught herself. Pam got mad as hell. She told Tim, I can help that you have a little dick; maybe it runs in the family, hell if I know. I do not have time for this fucking shit. Go find you a virgin because I am not one. That little dick of yours cannot start to get my pussy juices to running.

Tim tried to hit her but one of the bouncer grab him by his hand and threw him on the ground. The bouncer told Pam that he saw what was going on, on the cameras inside. He just could not stand to see a man jump on a lady. Pam told him thanks and she got in her car to go home.

Pam got home took a shower, read her bible, said her prayers and she went to bed. Pam woke up at 9am, fix her breakfast and she went to church. She decided to dress down because she got so tired of attracting fools.

Pam really enjoyed the preacher's message. He was talking about forgiveness and Pam thought about her mom, she knew that she had to forgive her mom for all the things that she did to her. Someone had to be the bigger person. Pam decided to take three days off and return home to see her mom. She returned home and she called all of her sibling and informed them that they had to let bygone be bygone. We have to forgive our mom if we want to make it into heavens. Tonya told Pam that Paula had gotten in touch with her and that she was married had a set of twin girls and worked as a Pharmacist. She began to serve the LORD and she had forgiven their mom years ago and that she was coming home to make amends.

Pam told Tonya that they needed to get together the following weekend and just be a family again.

Pam informed her Supervisor that she needed to take two days off with her weekend and her Supervisor told her that she was a very dependable worker and it would not be a problem.

Pam packed two suitcases full and rented a car. She arrived back to Memphis and all of her family was there. All of got together at their mom house and cooked a big dinner. Their mom finally came into the dining room and she asked what was going on. Pam started to talk first. She told her mom that she forgive her far the way that she treated her when she was younger and it was time to let go of the pass. Patty got very upset. She told Pam what the hell are you talking about, I am not doing a dam thing. I hate all of your asses. Get the hell out of my house and do not come back. I will never take your forgiveness. I hate I ever had you all. Get the hell out of my house and don't ever come back. Tonya got up and she told all of her siblings that she had to leave and she would never come back. Poor Kathy loved her mom and she could do no wrong. Kathy told Patty that she was not going anywhere and she was going to get through this and this too shall pass. Patty told Kathy to get her no good Sanctified ass out of here house and to lose her number and never return. I never wanted child and since you all are grown, I do not need you get the hell out!

Each sibling left to return home and they agreed to keep in touch. Each one said a prayer for Patty. Patty needed Jesus just like a tornado.

Pam made it back to Nashville. She sat there and just started to remember some of the things that her mom said and did to her. Patty never showed them any love. Pam could remember that when she was smaller each time that Patty would meet a new man she would load them in her car and follow the man. Paula never would go, she would call her father and he would come and get her. Their father tried to get the rest of them but Patty would put the pedal to the medal and just take off and John could not get the rest of his children out of the car.

There were many times they were left at the hotel while Patty would go off with whom ever. The only thing they had to eat was cereal and milk. They were so thin. Pam just wished that someone would come and get them and take them away. Patty always told them if they tell anyone about what is going on in her home she would kill them and kill herself.

Pam got to thinking about the time that her mom placed all of her siblings in the closet with this big rat inside of it. Each time they would cry. Tim got older and he finally killed that rat but Patty never knew. When she placed them inside of the closet, they would sneak in a candle and matches. They just started to have bible study in the closet. As Pam was thinking about her childhood she did not realize that she was crying. Pam raised her hands to the LORD to have mercy on her mom and she would turn her life over to him.

Pam finally decided that she just had to forget about those bad days when she was little and look on the bright side that each one of them made it and was alive. They did have issues but just kept on going.

Pam finally dosed off to sleep after saying her pray and she slept through the night without having any nightmares.

Her siblings call to say the same thing, so maybe the curse was over.

Pam went to church that Sunday and she really enjoyed herself. One of the Deacons came to her car as she was about to close the door. His name was Kenny. Kenny was a smooth chocolate brother. He was single without any children and thirty –three years old, had a Doctorate degree in Education, a big mansion that sit on top of a hill and fancy cars. He told Pam that he wanted to take her out and show her the town. Pam said to herself, something is not right with this picture. She told Kenny that she would like to think about it. Kenny got mad because he thought that because he had a doctorate degree and material things that Pam would just jump on his bandwagon. Pam had seen enough fools before and she just did not have time to be beat up, cussed out or stalked. Kenny turned back around and asked Pam could he just have her digits. Pam asked him, "What part of I will think about it that you do not understand? Kenny told her that she was the first female that had turned him down and he just did not like it. Pam told him to kiss her black ass when she has diarrhea and to go to hell quick and in a hurry on rollers skates.

Pam could see the veins in Kenny's neck. She said, here I go again dealing with a dam fool. I can't win for loosing. Pam just shut her door and took off. She said to herself, I am tired of this dam shit.

Pam got home; she got out of her clothes and then began to eat dinner. After dinner Pam decided to get the latest book by Mary Monroe to read it but her phone rang and it was she little brother Michael. Michael was sweet but we loved him. I remember my older brother told my mom that something was not right with Michael when he was two years. My mom got so mad. Michael used to love to dress up in Pennies' clothes. My mom did not try to explain it to him that little boys do not dress like that. As he got older he became more and more like a woman. I had to pray for him each day. I asked Michael what he wanted and he told me that he had turned his life over to the LORD and was so happy. That his Pastor prayed for him, gave him some scriptures out of the Bible to read on homosexuality. Michael, said, I know it was wrong to be that way. I am so glad that the LORD saved me. I have been taking the HIV test for years and so far I am negative. I want to get married and have children. Pam jumped up and shouted, just praising the Almighty GOD.

Michael went on to say that he had met this nice young lady and her name was Vicky. Vicky did not have any children, and she was a teacher. They decided to get married at the courthouse next week. Michael was so happy, he told Pam that she would let her know when the reception was going to be and he was going to call the rest of his sibling.

The next week came so quick. Michael and Vicky got married at the courthouse. Then they called their entire family to come to The Freedman Community Center. Everyone came except for Michael's mom. He was sad at first but the rest of the family told him that it was his day. The reception went well. Vicky told everyone to line up so that she could toss the bouquet. Pam reached for it for the heck of it but this young girl snatched it out of her hand and she scratched Pam. Before Pam knew it he had popped the young girl up side of head. The girl fell and dropped the bouquet. Pam told her young bitch for that I am going to take the bouquet from your young dumb ass because it will be a long time before you get married anyway.

People were just looking at Pam like she had lost her mind. Pam looked around and said, "Do anyone want some of this? Then the DJ said may the Bride and Groom approach the dance floor for your first dance. Then he said everyone get on the dance floor. Pam did not have anyone to dance with. Then all of a sudden there was a tap on her back. She looked around and there was the most handsome man she had ever seen. He had the smoothest skin, nice abs, white teeth, and a goatee and dressed to impress. He asked her name and did she want to dance. Pam told him that she hadn't danced in a lot time but will give it her best.

Dude had some good moves. They were in sync with each other. They danced most of the night. There were several females looking and rolled their eyes. Pam stuck her middle finger up and those by's turned their heads. Pam told him that she did not know his name and he said that his name was Paul and he was greedy and he wanted all of her. Pam told him to keep is boots on because she had just met him. She did not know anything about him. Paul told her that he was 33 years-old, single, no baby mama, a dentist with his own practice, a two-story home on 120- acres. Pam said, dam I am very impressed. He acted Pam what she did and she told him that she was an RN. He asked her for her number, she told him that she could not do that but she would take his number. Pam looked at her watch and it was eleven o'clock. Pam told Paul that she had to say goodbye to her family and head home because she had to give the LORD her time. Paul said, a woman who loves the LORD, I really like that. Paul asked her could he go to church with her, she told him that she would give him the address and he could Google it. Paul told her if you are scared say that you are scare. Pam told him she was not scared of anything or anybody but the LORD. Pam turned around to leave and Paul grabbed her hand. Pam rolled her eyes. Paul told her an eye roller huh. He told her that he was sorry. Pam accepted his apology. He asked could he walk with her to say goodnight to everyone. Pam told him no problem.

They said their goodbyes and Paul walked her to her car and they said good night.

Pam watched him in her rearview mirror and just shook her head and said, so fine. I just wonder what he got down below. I arrived at her Hotel in no time and she got ready for bed. She read her bible and said her prayers and lay down. Pam got up got ready and went to church. Paul was there waiting on her. Pam told him that he was prompt and she like that. They went into church together. One of the church members told her that this was the first time that she had seen her with a man at church. She to the lady that, she needs to have her mind on the LORD and not her.

Pam grabbed Paul's hand and led him to a seat. The preacher started to preach and people got to shouting. They had a great time. Paul asked her what was she doing after church. Pam told him that she had to pack to go back to Nashville. Paul told her that he thought that she stayed in Memphis. Pam told him that she has left Memphis to attend college. Paul told her that he stayed 15 minutes from Nashville and that was his sister that her brother had gotten married to. He was just her for her wedding. He also told her that he wanted to get to know her better.

Pam told him that she just wanted to take it slow. He asked could they ride back to Nashville together. Pam told him yes. Pam told her what Hotel she was in and she told him that she was just two doors down. He told her that he would pick her up in three hours but they needed to eat first.

Pam and Paul went out to eat. They ready enjoyed the meal. Paul decided to pay for both meals. Pam told him thank you. Pam asked him would he drop her all at the rental place so that she could return her car. Paul followed her to return her car. Then they were in route to the Motel. They said their goodbyes so that they could pack. Pam text all of her family to let them know that she was riding with Paul, Vicky's bother, how tall he was, shoe size, phone number and car tags number.

Paul and Pam left on time. They made a few stops so that they could stretch their legs. They finally made it to Nashville just as it was getting dark. Paul helped Pam with her luggage. Pam opened the door and she told Paul to place the luggage by the door. She asked him did he want any coffee and he said yes. They had coffee and a cinnamon roll. Paul told her that he hated to leave but he has a busy day tomorrow. He asked her could he just taste her lips and he said yes. They begin to kiss. Pam grabbed his buttock and Paul like that. He begin to moan. This his baby anaconda stretched out. Pam felt it next to her leg, she just had to feel. She told him such a huge one and do you know had to work that thang. He told her is not but one way to find out. She told him, dam, I would love too, my vagina wall are vibrating like a cell phone. Paul told her that he knew how to just fuck her and make that pussay erupt like a volcano. Pam told him that he just have to wait until they get to know each other better. Paul told her that he would have to go home and take a very long, cold shower. Pam smirked and she told him, I guess so. Paul gave her a peck on her left cheek and he told her that he would call her later.

Pam unpacked her bags and she said to herself that she had to get her a pet.

Pam went to work and her day was great. She did not have any problems out of any of her nasty old patients. She decided to go to Petco to look at different pets. When she walked into the door, she heard this Parrot talking. The parrot was say, I need to fuck, fuck, fuck. I am tired of being up in this cage. I need to soar oates and make a few babies. Pam could not do anything but laugh. She told the clerk that she would take the parrot. The clerk told Pam thank GOD, that parrot mouth is so foul and it is running away some of my best customers.

Pam paid for the parrot, got a few more items and she left. Pam and a parrot left. While they were driving, the parrot said, I want to listen to R. Kelly's song, I don't see nothing wrong with a little bump and grind. Pam just shook her head. She told the parrot, look I run this show, either you shut up or I will turn around and take you back to the store. The parrot said, yes ma.

Pam arrived home and she placed the parrot in the den so that she would not hear it thought out the night. The first night the parrot was sweet. Paul called and he asked could he come over. Paul came and he had take-out for them both. Paul entered the kitchen and he saw the cage. He took the covering off it. The parrot said what's up my brother? Paul said, o you can talk. The parrot said, yes. Pam came back into the kitchen and she told Pam that she had gotten herself into some shit with this parrot. The parrot said, oh Paul, I just know that you have a nice long penis and you know how to use that big, long round thank. If Pam get a hold of that she will not have to used that bullet in that drawer of yours. Pam turn red in the face. She said dam I am going to have to sit him outside to get a little air. There is a stray cat out there and he might just love to look at you. The parrot said, please, please don't put me out there. I hate cats, they always tries to eat me. The only cat I wouldn't care eating is yours because you will be my trick and I will sure treat that cat of yours right.

Pam had enough. She hung the parrot up on her back porch. The parrot pleaded and pleaded but Pam did not care. She took the parrot outside and decided to let it stay for thirty minutes. She heard it just hollowing but he did not care. She and Paul sat down to eat and the food was great. Then they went back into the living room to watch TV. Each talked about their family and then Pam walls were just pulsating. She did want to give up her goodies but she could not help it. She asked Paul did he have any condoms and he told her yes. She told him to go into the bedroom on the left. Paul went and he got comfortable. Pam came in with some whip cream and cherries. She told him that he was going to be her chocolate sundae. She got an old comforter and placed it on the bed. She told Paul to close his eyes and relax. She sprayed whip cream on his nipples, down his stomach, all over his penis and then she placed a cherry on top. She told him that he could open his eyes and he said dam, dam and dam.

Pam put some whip cream around his eyes and on his lips. She started from his eyes and worked herself down to the cherry on his penis. Paul was so excited. His penis stretched out to about twelve inches. He was so excited and he never felt this way before. He just could not take it anymore. He told Pam that he needed her to give him the whip cream. He sprayed the whip cream on both of her breast, down to her vagina and he placed four cherries on top of her pussay, He licked her from the front to the back. He placed the XXXL condom on his penis. He told her to relax, and he did. He enter her little by little. He finally ease all of it in, he pulled out and put it back in. Pam was in heaven. This went on for an hour. Pam had nutted at least six times. Then she felt and explosion like never before, she saw star and felt like the Fourth of July. Paul began to stream like a big old black bear. They came at the same time. Paul said, heart slow down! Slow down.

Pam said, dam, I have never felt this way before. I think that I am going to have to marry you. Paul said, you think. They both got into the shower and it started all over again. The both of them felt like a ragdoll and they could not make it to the bed. They just fell onto the carpet. About 30 minutes later they got up. Pam put on her robe and she went outside and got her parrot. The parrot was mad as hell. It told Pam, I know you and Paul were in there fucking really hard. I heard ya'll nasty asses. Pam told the parrot, do you want to stay out her all night? The parrot shook his head no. She brought it back it and it looked at Paul and just whistle but did not say anything out of place because it did not want to go back outside. It did have an encounter with the cat but it played dead. Then the cat just left. It remained quiet so that it could her all that moaning and groaning that was coming from inside the house.

Pam asked Paul did he want to stay the night since all the sex they had, it was late. Paul told her yes. The parrot said, "I know there is not going to be no more fucking under my roof." Paul just fell out on the floor laughing. He asked Pam, where did you get this talking mofo from? Pam told him that she had gotten lonely. Paul told her that she might just have to take it back. The parrot started talking, no! no! no! I do not want to go back to that place. I will try to do better but it is just hard. Pam placed the parrot in the garage so that they could not hear it.

Paul and Pam went to sleep. They slept so well since the parrot was not in the house. They both woke up early. Paul decided to cook Pam a nice breakfast. The both of them finished. Paul decided to go home to change and told Pam to come by his office so that they could go out to eat. Pam told him that it would be great and she did not want any shit out of any of his employees. Paul told her that it would not be a problem.

Pam finished up with her four patients and she arrived at Paul's practice tem minutes before twelve. She just want to get the feel of his employees. She walked in and there were not any patients waiting. The place was very nice, Pam was very impressed. Pam asked for Paul and when she did she notice one of the Assistant rolled her eyes. Pam asked her, do you have an eye problem and if you do you need to get them checked. Please do not rolled your eyes because it make you look really ugly. The employee put up her middle finger. Pam told her to fuck herself because she was going to fuck Paul tonight until he holler stop Pretty Momma. Pam told her to do her job and tell Paul that she was waiting on him. If she wanted to keep her job she would mind her own business. Pam looked at her name take and said, please to that Lashitta. Latrice told her to pronounce her name right or else she would mop her pretty ass on this floor. Pam told her that she might be pretty but she knew how to get a bitch off of her back.

Before they could go any farther, Paul finally came out. He kissed Pam on the cheek and he told his staff that he would be back at 1:30. Ask they were walking Pam turned around and told Lashitta that she was going to fuck Paul on his lunch break and gave her the middle finger.

Paul and Pam had a very good lunch. They arrived back at the office and he kissed her goodbye. He told her that he would see him tonight. Pam needed to use the bathroom. As she was watching her hands, Latrice came it and she was mad as hell. She told Pam, bitch, I have been after him for three years and you get him just like that. Pam told her hoe, I am a woman and you are a fucking hood rat.

Paul knows what he wants and evidently it wasn't you. Latrice pushed Pam. Pam told Latrice that it was on like a pot of neck bones. Pam kicked her in her stomach and when she bend over to grab her stomach Pam double up her hands and she popped Latrice in the top of her head and Latrice fell on the floor gasping for air. The Pam kicked her in her big old ass and left out of the bathroom.

Pam told the other Assistant that she had a sick co-worker on the floor in the bathroom. Pam left so that she could finish taking care of her patients.

Pam arrived home at 5 o'clock, took a shower and start making dinner. Paul arrived an hour later. Pam asked him how was the rest of his day? Paul told her that after she left he had to call 9-11 because Latrice got sick and was taken to the hospital. He closed the office early and went to check on her. The doctor in the ER told him that she would have to stay overnight due to she has a bruised stomach, a slight concussion and it looked like she was kicked in the ass. Pam told him that she was so sorry. Paul looked at her strange and he asked her did she know anything about the incident because his employee told that she told her that there was sick co-worker in the bathroom.

Pam told him yes and the reason why she did it. Paul just shook his head and told her that he do not want to get on her bad side. Paul also told her that he had to call her husband to let him know that she had gotten hurt at work. Pam said, "that chick is married." Paul told yes, with a set of three years old twins. Pam said I will be dammed. She told Paul that she said that she had been trying to get you for years. Paul told Pam that he thought that she was just honestly flirting with him but did not take it seriously.

Paul told her that she would to apply for workman comp. due to her being hurt on the job. Pam did not feel bad at all. They finished eating and went in to the living room. Paul asked where her pet parrot was. Pam told him that it was on the patio. Paul told her, oh, I have you all to myself. Pam told him that he sure did.

Paul took as shower and he asked Pam was she ready to ride his log all night? Pam told him yes. Pam went to the fridge and got some chocolate syrup and she placed it all over his penis. She told him that she was going to lick his chocolate log until he could not take it anymore. Paul began to feel so good, that thang swollen up so big. He told her that he could not take it anymore. Pam told him that she want him to take her from the back and he did. He eased that cock in and out, in and out. He was just teasing her. She told him not to play with her because she could get Eddie out of the drawer and if she want it like that. She told him to fuck her real, real hard. Paul told her if that is what you want I will get it to you.

Paul flipped and flopped her and Pam enjoyed it. Pam could feel the both of them getting ready to climax. Finally they both came and Pam fell off of the bed and bumped her head. He asked her was she okay and she told him no. Pam had as big goose egg on her forehead. She told him that she could not go to work like that. Paul told her that she could. He went to the kitchen and got some ice and placed it in a towel and told her to try to hold it there for ten minutes and it should help the swelling. He watched her most of the night until he finally went to sleep.

They woke up and the swelling had gone down some. Pam told him that they really did some wild fucking like an untamed animal. Paul told her that when he fuck her he does feel like a dog in heat and he just can't stop himself. She had the best puss say that he had ever fucked. Paul got up and he pulled a box out of his jacket and he got on one knee and he asked Pam would she do the honor of becoming his wife. Pam fainted and when she woke up, Paul was still beside her but he had her in his arms. Pam shook her head and asked him what had happened. Paul repeated himself and Pam said, yes!

## Pains and Triumphs

You know that living in the 70's was hard and lonely. My mom Wilma had six children and their names are: Sadie, Doris, Velma, George and Darla. Wilma never got married and all of her children had different daddies. Darla was the youngest and the Black Sheep of the family. Her entire family mistreated her all of her life.

Sometimes Darla wished that she had a different family. Growing up with five other siblings was a total nightmare. When I was about five years old I knew that I was different. All of my siblings called me black and ugly. I really didn't know that color I was because my mom never told me anything.

I was a very nosey child. I remember one time when I was able to go over to my Aunt's home. My cousins were talking about their boyfriends. They told me not to go into the front room and I did. I saw my Aunt and this man. I didn't know what they were doing but I knew that they were going up and down and up and down. I ran out because I didn't know what I was looking at. I decided to go back home. My mom told me to go to my room with my nosey self. I went outside and crawled under the house. I heard my sister Tina asked my mom why did she have me because I was the ugliest thing she ever seen. She really do not fit into our family. I wanted to cry so badly but I didn't.

As a small child, I knew that Jesus was in the mist of my life. The next day while I was under the house. I heard my mom say I know what I will do, I will get Mr. Lumpbone to build a room onto the back of the house. When Darla turns ten years old that is where she is going. I just wished I had a poke iron because I would poke all of them in their big butts.

The next day when I was at the back of the house playing. I heard my mom calling my name but I ignored her. A few minutes passed by and I came into the house. My mom asked me did I hear calling me and I said no mam. She slapped me upside the head and said, I wished I never slept with your no count daddy. I said, why did you and she slapped me again and I ran to my room. I said my prayers and went to bed.

The next day I had to go to school. It was my first day and I had a nice school teacher. Mrs. Jones told us to stand up and say our names. I told her mines and my sister's names also. Mrs. Jones called me to the side and she told me that she had all of my sisters in her class but none of them mentioned me. I didn't not say anything. That day was a very good day. I prayed that I caught on because I had to teach myself everything. Mrs. Jones asked me where my supplies for was school and I told her that my mom didn't buy me any. Mrs. Jones just shook her head. She left the room and came back with a tablet and pencil. I cried and she just hugged me. I felt so good because no one never hugged me. She gave me homework to take home.

I got home and began to do my homework and my mom came into the room. She asked me where I got that paper from. I told her that Mrs. Jones gave it to me and she said, from now on she can buy your supplies. She gave me a letter to give to Mrs. Jones the next day. I prayed went to sleep.

The next day, I gave Mrs. Jones the note that mama gave me and she just frown. She told me to say over and she would take me home. Mrs. Jones helped me with my homework every day and I was so glad. My mom got mad because Mrs. Jones was bringing me home a little late. She started making me do my chores before I ate anything. Sometimes I would be so hungry and my stomach sounded like thunder. I just prayed harder. Each day when I finished my chores, I didn't have but a little to eat. My sisters thought that it was so funny. I knew that this would not last always.

The next day we were waiting for the bus and Tina told me not to stand so close to her because she didn't want anyone to know that we were related. I stuck my middle finger up and her. She tried to hit me and I moved out of the way and she fell into a mud puddle. She ran into the house crying and I got on the bus.

When I came home my mom asked me what happen and before I could answer her, she hit whipped me with an extension cord. She told me that I was going to bed without eating any dinner. I said my prayers and went to sleep.

The next day I went to school and Mrs. Jones asked me why I was wearing long sleeves. I told her that I was playing outside and got bitten by mosquitos. I was so happy to be at school.

The years flew by and now I was in the fifth grade. Mom had finally told me that my room was ready. I didn't have a choice, so I packed up the few clothes that I had. George was the only sibling who would come to see me. He always brought me leftovers and I was grateful. My room wasn't too bad. I had a small kitchen and I already knew how to cook.

Sadie was married with two children and her husband worked at the Post Office. Doris was a Unit Manager. Tina was a stripper and pregnant. George was a Doctor. Velma ran away from home every Friday night and came back on Sunday's. Momma got so tired of calling the police so she sent her away.

There would be family gathering and I was never invited. I would crawl through the attic and I could hear everything that was said. Sadie thought that she was a pot of gold. Doris had changed and lot. She had a boyfriend that stayed with her. He stayed whipping that tail. Mom tried to tell her to throw that trash out but she would not listen. My mom always told them that she didn't take no shit off of their daddies because they knew that she would slice them like a piece of steak. She told Doris that she could move back home and that trash better not step foot on her property because she would shoot him between his legs.

All of a sudden everything got quite. Velma walked in ranting and raving, saying that these dam pains feels like a volcano is erupting. That chick was in labor. I heard mama tell Sadie to call Mrs. Temple. Mrs. Temple was too late. Velma had a 10 lbs. baby. I heard momma say, LORD have mercy on my heart, that baby is white. I heard a loud noise and I knew momma big ass had fainted. Instead of Mrs. Temple taking care of Velma and the baby. She had to take care of momma big lard ass. She finally came too and she still remembered that the baby was white.

Momma started letting Velma go out when she was fifteen years old, so what she expected. Velma knew that momma was getting her groove on so she did too. Six weeks had passed since Velma had that white baby. Momma finally gave in and she loved that baby. Momma came to the cloth line and told me to go to the mailbox. She said if I looked at the mail that she would knock my head off. I got the mail and there was a mail addressed to my mom and me. I looked to see was she looking and she was planting flowers. I folded the letter up and place it in my shoe. I took mom the mail and she looked through it and she asked me was this all of it and I told her, yes mam.

I went to my room and I opened up the letter and there was a check for 1500 dollars. I was so mad. All of the years, I had to wear second-hand clothes and hand me downs while my other siblings wore new clothes. The other children made fun of me. I remember one time I had this coat on and it was clean. One of the student asked me where I got that old lady coat from. I didn't say anything. I was so thankful that I had one.

Mrs. Jones wasn't my teacher anymore but I went to her room during recess. This day when I went to her room. I told her that I needed to talk to her. I told her how my family did me and she just cried and cried. I told her about the check and she took me to the bank and deposited the check into a Savings Account. She opened up a P.O. Box so that all of the mail could go there. She got me so better clothes. That day after school, my mom saw me with a bag and she asked me what was in there. I told her that Mrs. Jones bought me some clothes. She jerked the sack from me and she looked into it. Then she said, she got good taste. I wouldn't never spend that kind of money on your ugly ass.

I was so glad to get those new clothes but I had to do something about my hair. The next day I asked Mrs. Jones could she take me to the Beauty Shop and she did. The hair dresser finished my hair and she gave me the mirror. I could have fell out of the chair. My hair was beautiful and so was I. I thanked Mrs. Jones. The next day when I went to school, this girl came up to me and she said, so you think you pretty now! I told her, yes I do. She tried to hit me so I popped her in her belly and when she grabbed her belly. I balled both of my hands and I hit her in the top of her head and she fell to the floor. The Principle came over and she told me that she was so glad that I finally stuck up for myself. From that day on no one messed with me.

Later that evening my brother George came to my door. I was kinda scare to let him in. I let him in but was really scared. He told me not to worry because our mother had gone shopping. He told me that he was so sorry for mistreating me all of those years. He also said that he did not know why we called her momma because she never was. I told him that I did not hate them because the Bible teaches not to hate anyone. We became friends after that. George started to come to see me more often and brought me food and clothes. He told me that he got the money from momma and she would not miss it because she had so much.

The years flew by and I am 18 years old and it was time for me to graduate from high school. I gave my mom an invitation to my graduation and she just tore it up. On graduation night the only people who showed up were Mrs. Jones and George. I was happy to see them. I was at the top of my class and received several scholarships.

Tina never returned home, she got married and moved to California. Velma was living in Jamaica with her lawyer husband. She finally told him that he was the father. Doris was living in Africa working as a Director of Nursing at the largest hospital there. She finally meet Mr. Right and he was the Hospital Administrator. They had two boys and a girls. Poor Sadie had just lost her mind. She had to be admitted into a mental institution. Her high society life drove her crazy and plus her husband had ran away with the babysitter.

I tried to call George because I wanted to thank him for being so good to me. George had finally decided to move in with his girlfriend of two years. She wanted to get married but he wasn't ready. George and his girlfriend stayed in Atlanta. I called and called but still couldn't get him, so I called his job. George worked as a doctor at Emory Hospital. I finally got in touch with his Supervisor. He told me that he was so sorry for my lost and that George and his girlfriend were murdered. Someone torched their placed and his lawyer need to talk to me. He gave me all of the necessary information.

I told my family and we decided to drive to Atlanta. The funeral was so sad. The police was there because they hadn't found the murderer/murderers. After the funeral was over, we all went to the lawyer's office. The lawyer told me that he had left me 3 million dollars, his car and his home. He also told me that his home was paid for and if I wanted to say in it, I could or sell it. I told him to sell it and send me the check. I thanked him and left. My family was so mad, I didn't care. They told me to get back to Tennessee the best way that I could. I purchase me a ticket from the Greyhound Bus Station.

I was so glad to be back home. My mom came to my room and told me that I had three days to move or be evicted by the Sheriff Department. She was still mad because George left everything for me. I used my mom's phone to call Mrs. Jones to ask her could I move in with her and she told me yes. I got a cab and left. I stayed with Mrs. Jones until I was able to go to college. Mrs. Jones taught me how to drive and she took me to the bank. She gave me all of my banking information. I had over a million dollars into my Savings Account. I transferred 50,000 in to my Checking Account. Mrs. Jones took me to my first car. I was so thankful.

It was finally time for me to attend college. I decided to go to the University of Tennessee for a Physical Therapist. I said my goodbyes to Mrs. Jones and decided to stop to get some gas before I left. I went to pay for my gas and this gentleman asked who I was and I told him. He said I kind of figured that. I just looked at him and he told me that he needed to talk to me. He told his son to take over and we went into his office. He informed me that I was his niece. He also told me that his brother raped my mom and his dad sent him away. I didn't not want to believe it but he just knew too much. He asked me where was I on my too and I told him. He gave me a check for 100,000 for my education. I told him that I had a full scholarship but he told me to take it anyway. I hugged him and thank him and continued on my journey.

I really enjoyed going to college and just stayed to myself. The years flew by and I was accepted as a Physical Therapist at Methodist Hospital. I found me an apartment. Mrs. Jones came by to visit me. She told me that she was going to London for three years to help her daughter with her grandchildren and that she would stay in touch. Mrs. Jones also told me that she had sold her home and fifty acres of land. She gave me a Cashier Check for 150,000. I told her that her kindness during all those years were worth more that money and that she was like a mother to me. She told me that she had already adopted me as her child in her heart. I just cried.

I was still in Orientation and I had to work with this guy named Daryl. He was my trainer. He tried everyday to take me out but I refused each time. I was new and some people think because you are new that you can be easily used. I was so glad that Orientation was over and that I could start to work with others. Daryl continued to try to talk to me and we finally went out and we really had a good time. We continued to talk and began dating. I was told by my supervisor that she had to change my hours. I didn't tell Daryl. I was came in and I overheard one of the Nurses talking to Daryl. She asked him why he was talking to me with my ugly self. He told her the only reason he was talking to me is because he heard that I had a lot of money and he was going to get some of it.

The money that I had was mines and no one was going to get it. I continued to see him and then he asked me to load him so money to get some tires to put on his car. I told him do I look like a dam bank. He got mad and tried to break my arm. One of the Supervisor saw him to let me go. He told Daryl that he could have him fired. He asked me was I okay and I told him yes. I went to the ER and got checked out. I was okay but a little sore. Daryl was transferred to another hospital.

Two years later I meet Clarence while I was getting off. He was a good looking man. He was a doctor. We started talking and he was very nice. He started giving me gifts and I continued to take them. One day while I was working with a patient, I got a phone call. The person on the other end told me to leave her husband alone and I told her to tell him to leave me along. She got mad and hung up.

Clarence and I went to dinner that night and I asked him was he married and he told me no. I knew that he was lying. I continued to date him. The next day my Supervisor gave me a letter. I opened it and there was a clipping with a copy of marriage license with Clarence and his wife names on it. I show it to him and he told me how sorry he was. We stopped talking. I just spent a lot of time during overtime.

One day while I was at work and I just started to feel sick. I ran into the bathroom. The door opened and this Nurse came in and she act me what was wrong. I told her that I had been working so much overtime and just was tired. She told me to me to go to the doctor to be on the safe side. I left work and got a pregnancy test. I followed the instructions and yes I was pregnant. I didn't cry. The next day while I was at work, I asked one of the doctors could he recommend me a Family Doctor. I made an appointment.

I went to the doctor and was told that I was about two months pregnant. I went home and I cried and cried. When I finished crying, I was still pregnant. I called Clarence and asked him could he come over and he agreed. He came over an hour later. I told him that I was pregnant by him and with twins. He asked me who the father was and I just couldn't believe. He was the first guy I had been with sexually. He called me all kinds of names. I picked up the cordless phone and hit him upside the head. I told him to kiss my ass up to my aorta and get the hell out of my house.

Clarence started dodging me at work. I didn't care. I had a baby to take care of. I had to go back to the doctor and I was about three month pregnant. I was given an ultrasound and the doctor told me that he heard two heart beats. I left and drove around. I asked the LORD what I was going to do. A voice said, everything will be okay. I knew that it would. My stomach started growing and growing. Many of my co-workers were happy for me whereas, so were not. I did not care. I was given a baby shower and how so much stuff until I had to rent a van to deliver them home.

I was just sitting at home one day with my swollen feet propped up. My doorbell rang. I opened it up and there was a female standing there. She asked could she come in and I told her yes. I knew who she was. She sat down and she told me that she knew that I was pregnant by her husband. I wasn't the first woman that he dated and would not be the last. I was first one to claim to be pregnant by him. I told her to get her musty ass out of my apartment before I call the police. She told me don't think that you will get child support because you will not. I told her that I didn't need her husband money because I had my own. She finally left.

The next day, I was just getting ready to go for a walk and the doorbell was rang. I opened the door and low and behold there stood my some of my family. They just hugged me and cried. They told me how sorry they were for mistreating me all of those years. Sadie was doing great and was married again. My mom had changed and now was married to a preacher. Sadie told me that she had something to tell me. She asked me did I remember old man Jim Jenkins and I told her no. She told me that when she was about fourteen years old, she was in the barn looking at the horses. Mr. Jim came in and he raped her. She said that she got pregnant and she tried to hide it.

She said that she went in labor. Her mom came into the room and wanted to know what all the noise was. She opened the door and saw a baby on the floor. I told her what had happened. She told me that we had to keep it ourselves and make like the baby was hers. She told me that is the reason she went crazy and had to get help. She also asked the LORD to forgive her.

I asked her how they found out that I was pregnant. She told me that Daryl knew her and they got to talking. She just knew that it had to be me. We decided to stay in touch.

Two weeks later, I was in the hospital delivering my twins. I named them Shantale and Danielle. My entire family came to see me after the twins and I came home. Each stayed a week a piece until I had to go back to work. I really didn't want to return. I finally found a babysitter next door. Ms. Thelma was a very nice woman. One day while she was getting the twins ready for me to take them home. She told me that she had three children, all boys. Todd was the worst child that she had. One night he got drunk and he hit and embankment. He was thrown out of the car. He got up and he saw the car going across the field. He ran after the car and called the care a son of a bitch. From then on he stopped drinking. I got the twins and left.

I got my mail and put the twins in their playpen. I saw this letter from my family. I was scared to open it. When I did, there was a check for 350,000. There was a letter explaining how sorry they were for mistreating me all of those years. I was so blessed. I put the money into a trust fund for the twins.

One of my co-workers introduced me to this guy named Kenny. We started talking but I was going to take it slow. Kenny and I dated for about eight months before, I let him come over to the house. The twins were two years old now and they seem to warm up to him. On New Year's Eve, we decided to meet up at B.B. Kings. Some co-workers and I left to go. We were having a great time. I finally spotted Kenny. I walked up to him and he asked why I was here. I told him that he invited me. He told me that he did not have time for my lies and he walked off. I went back to my co-workers and they asked me what had happened. I told them. I looked around and I saw him with another female. Maxine one of my co-workers told me that she would go over there and kick him dead in his ass. I told her that it was worth it. We drank our Long Island Tea and partied with these good-looking brothers. Maxine hit it off with Dewayne, Teresa with Paul and I hit it off with Roger. Roger kissed me on my cheek and my panties got wet. I didn't want to leave but I knew that I had to get home. The night was winding down and we exchanged numbers. I got home and it was almost 2pm. So I didn't bother Ms. Thelma. The next day I did go and pick up my babies. Ms. Thelma asked me did I have a good time and I told her that I did.

I didn't call Rodger because I did not want to seem that I was desperate. Two weeks past and Roger finally called me to ask could he take me out and I told him that he could. Ms. Thelma was glad to take care of the twins. Rodger came over but Shantale hit behind me but Danielle said hi and she ran and grabbed my leg. I knew something was up. You have to pay attention to the children. Rodger and I went out and it was nice.

We continued to date and he spent a lot of money on me. One night I decided to go over to his house. He was kissing me and I continue to push him off. I just wasn't into it. He was a sloppy kisser. He got mad and said bitch you are going to give it up tonight or else. He tried to pull my pants off and I kicked him in his mid-section. I tried to get out of the door but he pulled me by my hair and I tried to fight back but it wasn't any use. He got me and threw me in the trunk of his car. I don't know where he was going with me. I began to recite the 23 Psalms. The car finally came to a stop. He took me out and threw me on the ground with my purse. I laid there and played like I was dead until he drove off. I did get his Divers License number.

I started to walk. There was a car behind me. I took off running because I thought Roger was coming back to get me. Then heard someone say it's the police please but your hands up. I just fell in the street. I looked up and it was a Police Officer. I just fell out again. When I woke up, I was in the hospital. There was a Detective sitting at the foot of my bed. She asked me what had happened. I told her and she left. Ms. Thelma came in with the twins and I was so thankful. The doctor came in and told me that I could go home but not to work. He would make sure that my Supervisor get the necessary information. I was so sore but was glad to go home. Ms. Thelma told me that she would see to the twins until I felt better. I got home and looked in the mirror, my face was so swollen and I looked like the Hunch Back of Norte of Dame.

I was just sitting around and then the doorbell rang. There were two Detectives at my door. I let them in. They told me that they ran the tags and Roger had a rap sheet about a foot long. They told me that I was lucky and that they had been looking for Roger a long time. They also told me that there was a reward. I told them to donate the money to the Abuse Shelter. They told me that I number 204. They told me that I was the first one that he did not get a chance to rape because I fought back. After they left I just got on my knees and thank the LORD.

The swelling had finally gone down and I was ready to return to work. I got back to work and my co-worker were so glad to see me. One of the Nurses wasn't so happy to see me and I didn't care. I was in the breakroom fixing my lunch and she came in and she told me I heard about what happen to you and I don't feel sorry for your ass. I told her that I didn't give a shit and if she kept fucking with me I was going to beat her ass like she stole something. She put her middle finger up, I grabbed it and heard it snapped. She ran out of the bathroom hollering. Later I found out that she had to have a surgery and would be out for two months. I was glad.

As I was getting ready to go home, this male Nurse asked me could he take me out and I told him hell no. He pushed me into one of the empty rooms and tried to take it. I got the phone and hit him upside his head and left him there. I went home. The next day when I came to work they told me that the nurse was in ICU. I didn't feel bad. I just continued to do my job.

Both Nurses finally came back to work and they stayed out of my way. I was in the hallway and the male nurse saw me coming and he just holler and fell into the floor. Several nurses and doctors came running. They asked me what happened and I told them that I didn't know. Some said maybe he came back to work too early. I didn't have to worry about his ass anymore.

I got off work, pick-up the twins and just was getting ready to read a book and the doorbell rang. I asked who it was and the person said Jim Watkins. I let him in. I said to myself this old buzzard better not try anything do I was going to beat his ass. He asked me could he have a seat. I told him that he could. He told me that he was my father and he was so sorry for raping my mom. He said that she looked so enticing, he just had to have her. When his father found out about it he sent him away. He tried to make it up to me by sending me Child Support each month.

He hung his head down and told me that the reason that he was here was because he just had six months to live. He just wanted to see us before he goes to glory. He said that he had already asked the LORD for forgiveness. He said that when he left all those years, he found a nice older lady and he married her. She died over a year ago and he didn't want to get married. He said that I am 78 years old now and I want you to have everything. He said that he had a 100 acre ranch, 2 story house with a three car garage, four bedrooms and four and half baths. He also said that there was 500 million dollars in a trust fund that I would be able to get until I turned 25. There was 250 million that I could get at the time of his death. I ran over to him and just hugged him.

He asked could he see the twins and I went and got them. He played with them until they got sleepy and I put them to bed. He asked me how old they were and who the father was and I told him. He was kind of upset about Clarence but it was okay. He hugged me and left.

He came by each weekend for three months. The twins were now four years old and they were glad to see their Papa. I knew something was wrong when he did not come the following weekend. I went to work but was a little down. My work phone rang and it was a woman. I got this funny feeling and I just knew something was wrong. She told me who she was and why she called. She told me that all the funeral arrangements were made and the funeral would be in two days. I called my family and they told me that they would be there.

The funeral wasn't too sad. I got a chance to meet some of my father's family. Some were happy to see me whereas some weren't. I didn't care but my father's brother and his family made welcome. They told me to bring the twins by some Sunday's for dinner or stay the weekend. I told him that I would love to. We all said our goodbyes.

Two weeks later, my father's attorney came by and gave me the necessary papers. I decided to rent the apartment to Ms. Thelma's daughter and she rented hers to her son. We all moved to my father's home in the country. I took a month off from work to get settled in.

The time flew and it was time for me to return to work. My co-workers were so glad to see me and it was likewise. I was on my way to the bathroom and I saw Daryl. I was shocked. He pulled me by my arm and I pinched the shit out of him. He let me go. He told me, I heard that your old daddy died and left you millions. I knew your ass was a half-bred. I just did not have time for his mess. I took my ink pin out of my pocket and stuck him in his hand and told him not to ever touch me again. He called me a crazy bitch while trying to stop his hand from bleeding.

An hour later, I was sitting at my desk trying to finish my paperwork. I looked up there stood this fine ass doctor. He came close to me and ask me where you have been all of my life. I told him none of his dam business. He laughed and walked off. I got up and went to the bathroom because my kitty cat was on fire. I had to sit on the commode in order for it to get some air. I finally cooled down and went to wash my hands. The door opened and low and behold there walked in a stinky ass Shelly. She said, I see you met fine ass Dr. Paul Jones. I finished washing my hand and tried to leave the bathroom but I could. Shelly tapped me on my shoulder and I asked her what the hell she wanted. She said didn't you hear me. I didn't answer, I just socked her in her right eye and walked out of the bathroom. I heard her say, bitch my eye better not be swollen or your ass is grass and I am the lawnmower. I finished my work and went home.

Everyday for three months Dr. Jones just had to come to my office and stare. I finally asked him what the hell he wanted. He told me that he wanted to lick me like a lollypop. I was speechless. He asked me could he take me out to dinner. I told him no that he couldn't but he could come by my house and get a home cooked meal. He asked me for my address and I gave it to him.

I got home and I told the Cook if she didn't mind could she prepare some Soul Food. The Cook did and everything smelled so good. Dr. Paul arrived, I introduced him to the staff and my family. We sat down to eat. After we finished, we sat in the den. Paul started to ask me how I got my house because he knew that I couldn't afford it on my salary. I paused and I told him to get the fuck out of my home and he left. Ms. Thelma came in and she asked me what had happen and I told her and she said, "dam fool."

I was at work and Dr. Paul told me how sorry he was. He asked could he take me out to eat and start all over again. I told him that I would give him a second chance and if he fuck up this time he can go to hell on roller-skates quick and a hurry. Paul told me that he would pick me up around 6:30 pm.

I got home and told everyone. Ms. Thelma use to be a beautician so she fixed me up. My children pick out a nice dress for me. I finished getting dress, walked downstairs. Shantale, Danielle said that I looked like Cinderella. The doorbell rang and it was Paul. He looked at me so hard, I told him to get his jaw up off of the floor. We went to Olive Garden, the food was delicious. We talked and we talked but he never brought up how I could afford the house.

We made it home around 10:30 and Paul walked me to the door. He kissed me on my cheek and we said goodnight.

While at work in my office, Paul came by and he asked me could he take me to lunch and I said sure. Over lunch Paul told me that he stay with both of his parents because they were very old. He also said that he was the only one not married out of five siblings. I told him about my twins. We were just minding out own business when Shelly walked up to the table. She spoke to Paul but not to me. As she was passing she kick my leg and I punched her in her nose. She saw the blood and she fainted. Her uniform dress flew up and he had the crotch cut out of her draws. MRT was called, assessed her and she had a broken nose. While on the stretcher, she told me that she was going to kick my ass. I ignored her. Paul just looked at me and shook his head. He told me that I need to register to be a fighter because I keep abusing people. I told him to kiss my ass up to my Aorta. I was called into the office to do an incident report. I wrote down everything and was sent home for three days. I really did not care.

Paul and I continued to talk and he told me that he had to keep his guard up around me. I just looked at him and smiled. We had been talking for about eight months, so I decided to drop my drawers. Paul called and asked me could I come over and I told him yes. I arrived at his home about an hour later. He let me in and his pole was standing at attention. I could wait, so I held it until we got into his bed room. He put on a condom. We engaged in a little foreplay, I sucked both of his nipples and he was so excited. He kicked both legs into the air like he was riding a bike. We had sex eight times before I left to go home and old Sally was completely satisfied. Paul called me to make sure that I made it home okay and he told me that my sex was so good, I could bottle it and sex it for millions. I told him that he was crazy and he hung up.

As the weeks past, Paul and I continued to see each other. The sex was off the chain. One day while I was at work, I looked up and I saw this lady rolling her eyes at me. I just ignored her. Later on Paul came by to check on me and I told him about the little incident. I described the woman to him and he said that he didn't know her. I just said, okay.

The next day while was assisting a patent, Shelly came up to me and she stilled looked fuck up. She told me that she hadn't forgotten about what I had done to her and payback is a mother. I just let her talk but in the process, I was recording her all of the time. She told me, yes you think that you have Dr. Paul to yourself but you don't he has been dating this chick name Annie for some time. I told her thanks for the information. When she left, I took the recording to my Supervisor and he called Shelly's Supervisor in. She listened to the recording and said, she really have it in for you. I told her that I never did anything to her and the only thing I could think of is that she wanted Dr. Paul. Both Supervisor looked at each other and they burst out laughing. My Supervisor said, that what it is. She said that Dr. Paul had been around and that I would soon find out about him sooner or later. I got up and let to office so that I could complete work.

I got home and the twins were so excited to see me. I was so happy to see them also. We talked, they did their homework and got ready for bed. While I was reading, the phone rang and it was Paul. He told me that he needed some air and that I just wanted sex too much. I told him that the sex was good but if he wanted some air he would have all that he wanted and I hung up the phone.

As time went on, Paul went his way and I went mines. I was in the bathroom one day and this same chick was rolling her eyes at me. I said, to myself her we go again. I asked her what the fuck she wanted. She told me that she was tired of Dr. Paul not having enough time for her and her baby. Before she could say another word, I told her that she was rolling her eyes for nothing because Paul and I are not an item anymore. She told me that I was lying and I told her whatever. As I was leaving the bathroom, my head snapped back, she had a hold of my pony tail. I said to myself, I am so tired of beating these bitches ass. I pushed myself back into her and we were at a stall, I turned towards her and used both of my arms came up with my thumb and hit her under the chin. She let go of my hair. I took my belt off and made a loop around her hands and escorted her to my Supervisor. I told my Supervisor, that I was so tired of these women trying to whip me over Dr. Paul. My Supervisor called Security and escorted the woman to her car. Come to find out, she didn't even work here.

I got home and was in bed. I heard this voice said, get up and go over to Paul's house. I got dressed and I did. I parked my car beside the road and got out. I saw this car in the driveway. I knocked on the day and the same female that I had an encounter with answered the door. I was ready for her. I asked her where Paul was and she told me that he was in the bedroom. I pushed passed her and went into his room. There he was in the bed asleep with nothing but his shorts. I started drooling. He looked so good lying there. I touched him on his big toe and called his name. He said how in the hell did you get in to my house? I told him that I knocked and was let in by is woman. He told me just wait until I put my pants on, I am going to beat your ass. I took off running and got in my car. I rolled my window down a little. He tried to put his hands inside of the car. He told me that he was going to choke my ass. I got my knife and told him that if the wanted his finger he better move them out of my car. He did and while I was leaving he threw rocks at my car. I jumped out of my car and I told him that he had messed up. I got my bat out of my car and I hit him on his left arm and then his left hand. I knew that I had broken both. I got in my car and left.

The next day, I was off and there were two Policemen at my door. I let them in. They started asking me question about where I was last night. I told them that I was at home. He told me that Dr. Paul was assaulted last night and that my name was given by him and his wife. I told them that they had to be lying because I had been home all night. Ms. Thelma came from the kitchen and they started questioning her. They asked her what time did I get home and did I leave during the night. She told them that I had been at home all night. Both cops looked at each other and they left. Ms. Thelma asked me what the hell is going on. I wrote everything down and she just burst out laughing. I didn't want to talk in case they had placed a bug in my home. I called a friend of mines to debug my home and he came by and sure enough there were two bugs under my couch.

I went back to work and all eyes were on me. I just continued to do what I was hired to do. My day went by smoothly without incident. As I was walking to my car, I was approached by this officer. He asked my name and I told him, he gave me a piece of paper and said, you have been served. I read the paper, it stated that I was being sued for one million dollars. I had to appear in court in two weeks.

The two week rolled around for me to go to court. Dr. Paul and his so called wife were across from me. My attorney was a friend of my fathers and the Judge was my uncle. I know it was bias but what the hell. Dr. Paul was called first and he went into details what I supposed to have done. He was crying and was still in a cast. Then they called his so call wife and she told the same story. I was finally called. I told the court, that I don't know what they were talking about because, I was at home that night. My nanny and the rest of my staff were called also and they told the court that I was so sweet and wouldn't hurt a fly unless it was bothering me. Dr. Paul hollered out that I was a very abusive women and I had cause bodily harm to several co-workers. I just shook my head. The jury went to their chamber and they came back thirty minutes later and said not guilty due to not enough evidence. We all hugged each other. I looked over at Dr. Paul and he had his other hand like a gun. I mouthed, do fuck with me or I will be your other arm. I was so tired of beating folks' asses until I just did know what to do.

I was so glad to get back to work. Shelly no good ass decided to approach me. I had my antenna up. She sat at my desk and told me that she was so sorry for the way that she treated me and she wished that we could be friends. I told her that I had to soak my ass in bubble bath and think about that shit. She told me that she understood.

She apologized so much and we started slow. I told her do not fuck with me because I don't want to have to put my foot up her ass. We did become friends and I enjoyed her company. We had a lot in common. This new nurse came in and we all became friends.

About three months into our friendship, Betty did not come into to work and that was strange. We tried calling her house but we didn't get an answer. Shelly and I decided to call the police. We just couldn't sit around and not do anything. So, we got permission to leave and check on her. The police were there and it was roped off with yellow tape. The policeman did not want to let us in but I just had to see her. We walked in and the smell was awful. The policeman gave me a note read. It said, that she was glad to get to meet me and that she wanted to for so long. She was so sorry for killing my brother and his girlfriend. She was jealous of my brother and his girlfriend. She wanted him but he rejected her and she could not take it. I broke down in the house and I had to be carried out. I called my family and we had to relive his death over again. We were so glad for the closure.

One night when I got off of work and was getting into the car. Someone grabbed me by my hand and I pushed the panic button. The Security Guard came running. The gentleman told me that he was so sorry for scaring me. He told me that he was Betty's brother and he just wanted to apologized for what she had done. He dropped a bomb when he told me that Betty did have a child and he was my brothers. I told him about the letter but he said that my brother did date her for a while because he had seen them together. He told me that the child was five years old and he just wanted him to meet his other side of the family. I continue to look at him and he was such a cute man. He asked me could we get together and discuss their nephew. I told him that I would have to tell my family and I would call him.

I got home and I call my family and they were so happy. The next weekend we decided to meet in the park. He was kind of shy but when he saw the rest of the children, he was okay and he ran off to play. We found out that Betty had left her son a Trust Fund and who ever decided to take care him would not have to worry about his financial needs. We talked and I enjoyed his conversation. He asked me could he call me sometimes and I told him of course.

We did start out slow. He told me that his name was Ramone and he was from Cuba and he was half Black and Cuban. He also told me that he was a doctor and he worked for Methodist University. I told him that I work there also and that I did not need to have any issues with any of those hussies trying anything because I do not play fair.

Shelly came to me and told me that she had meet someone and I told her the same. We decided to double date and they were to pick us up at Shelly's house on Friday. I decided to go over her house early. I knocked on the door but did not get an answer. Shelly had told me on several occasions where her extra set of keys were. I got the key and went inside. It was stuffy in there and there was a foul odor. I called her name but did not get an answer. I walked into her bedroom and there she was in the bed but a pillow was on her head. I took off running and fell three times before I could get outside to my car. I called 9-11 and waited until they came. They told me to wait outside. Ramone and Carl drove up and asked me what was going on. I told them and Carl fainted. The cops had to call an ambulance for him. The cop came and he told us that she was smothered with a pillow. I was so stunned. Shelly and I had become friends. I just grabbed Ramone and cried on his shoulder. There was a powerful surge from Ramone and my Kitty Cat, I had to step back. Ramone decided to drive me home and he called one of his drivers to drop off my car. Poor Carl had to be taken to the hospital.

When I arrived home the nanny and the twins were outside playing. Ms. Thelma asked me what he matter and I told her. I call-in to work to let them know what happened to Shelly and I decided not to got to work. Ramone came and sat beside me. He was a nice catch. I know one thing, I had fallen asleep and Ramone was still there holding me. I told him that he could go and sleep in the quest room. The next morning, we had a feast. Ms. Thelma told me that he was a keeper. Ramone left and told me that he would call me.

Shelly family came by and told me when the funeral. They also told me how much Shelly appreciated me for forgiving her and becoming her friend. Ramone and I went to the funeral and it wasn't sad. After the funeral, Ramone, myself and the twins decided to go to visit my mom. My mom and her husband were so glad to see us. My mom called all of my sibling. I didn't know that they were all so close. We all decided to stay the night. The next day we went to church and when we came home we all cooked a home cook meal. My entire family just fell in love with him. I knew that he was a keeper. The twins really liked him. Later that evening, Ramone and I went to visit my Uncle on my father's side. When I arrived, my uncle and his wife were sitting on the porch. As we approached the porch, the both of them came and hugged us. She called some of my cousins and we ate fried pies and homemade ice-cream. My aunt told me that they were so glad to see me and not to be a strange. My aunt gave me a letter and told me not to open it until I got home and was by myself. I told her okay and thanks. We left with some fried pies and a bucket of her homemade ice-cream.

We arrived back home and Ramone kissed me goodbye. I hated to see him go. The twins and I got ready for bed. As I was lying there, I decided to open up the letter. The letter said that if anything happens to them that I would get, 3,000 acres of land, 12 houses and a 600-million-dollar Trust Fund to be divided with the twins. I just laid there, thank GOD and cried. I decided to donate some of my money to charity.

Time passed and Ramone and I became close. Ramone called and asked me could he come over. I told him yes. He entered the house and called Ms. Thelma and the twins. He asked them for my hand in marriage and I jumped up and said, yes.

Two weeks later we had a big wedding. My entire family was there. Eight month later, we had a set of triples. Since Ramone had custody of our nephew, he became our son also. Ramone and my family had a happy ending. I finally got my man without having to beat a bitch ass.

# Chapter One

Gloria

Gloria was a call girl. She was her own pimp. She wasn't giving her hard earned money to anyone else. She didn't fuck nothing but doctor's lawyers, principals, judges, senators. She had to get to doctor's office one day before work. Dr. Davis was very handsome. All of the nurses at the office wanted him but he didn't like to mix business with pleasure. Dr. Davies came into Gloria's room and asked her what, could he do for her? She told him that she had an itch that needed to be scratched. Gloria had cut the crotch out of her drawers and she opened her legs, then she told the doctor to take a look. He got an eye full. He told her to get her hot ass off of the table. She told him not until he scratched her itch. Dr. Davis started sweating. Gloria told him that it would not bite. It has been said that she had snapping turtle. Dr. Davis was so embarrassed. He began to think. Well. I haven't scratched anybody's itch in two years and it is about time. He gave Gloria his cell phone number.

Gloria and the doc started to date. She had his nose wide open. She did things to him that has never been done to him before. She loved to suck his nipples. That just drove him wide and he bucked just like a horse. They dated for a year and then he told her that she was too much for him. Gloria told him that it was fine with her and there was skin off her ass.

# Chapter Two

Gloria's next prop:

Gloria went to court the next month. She saw this handsome lawyer and the nice looking judge. She knew that when she left the courtroom, she would not have to pay that ticket. Instead she would have the judge and lawyer eating out of the palm of her hand. The judge asked her to rise and how did she plea? She told him that she was guilty of speeding 10 miles over but not 45 miles over the speeding limit. The judge asked the cop was she speeding and he said yes. She also told him that he did not have enough dick to put out her fire but his boss could. The judge called him to her desk and said meet me in my in chambers. He called a 30 minutes recess.

The judge and Gloria went into his chambers and the judge locks the door. He flipped out his long rod and asked her did he have enough dick for her? Gloria told him, what a find dick you have. The judge asked her could he put her fire out. She told him all day, every day. She told him that if he got into her Prada pocked book, he would have to write her a check for 30,000 and no one would know except them. She judge said okay. Gloria got the check. She told the judge to drop those drawers! She licked his nipples, around his neck, nibbled his balls and the judge got very excited. She backed that thang up and fucked the shit out of the judge. His head piece fell off of his head. He started screaming to the top of his lungs. He told him that, baby this is the best fucking I have had in ten years, so can we do this again. She told him yes and she gave him her phone number. The judge went into his private bathroom and fixed himself up. The judge and Gloria went back in the courtroom and the judge said this case is dismissed. The Rent-A-Cop was made as hell and he knew that the judge had gotten that hot pussy. Gloria looked at him and winked her eye. When she passed the cop, she pinched him on his butt and reminded him that he was not the boss.

While leaving the courtroom, this lawyer came up to her and he told her to give him what she had just given the judge! She told him, are you calling me a WHORE. He said no. She told him the time and the place. He gave her his card, she took it and she said thank Derrick.

Gloria called him a week later and he invited her to his home. He did have a beautiful home. She told Derrick that she was a call girl, she was her own boss and she charged 10,000 a trick. He said what! He told her that he needed to sample that thang before he paid that kind of money. They started to kiss. Gloria put whip cream all over his body and licked ever inch of him. She sucked that dick just like it was a lollypop and nibbled on his balls. He was screaming and hollering. He told her that her pussy was worth 50,000. She told him to sit on the couch, while she wrapped her legs around his waist. She rode him until his body felt like it was on fire. He yelled, put my fire out and please put my fire out! She didn't stop until he got his nut. He gave her the 50g' and begged her to see him again. She told him to call her.

They and they fuck, fuck and fuck. He told her one night that his heart was hurting. She thought that he was talking about is dick being hard. He kept clutching his chest. He told her to dial 9-11 because he was having a heart attack. Gloria said what the hell! She told him that she needed her money before he died. He wrote her a check and he fell over. Gloria knew CPR. She started administering CPR. He began became alert. She called 9-11, cleaned up, pulled the condom off of his limp dick and she left. She called the next day but the nurse wouldn't give her any information due to HIPPA. Gloria decided to go to the hospital to check on Derrick. Gloria entered the room; he looked at her and told her to get out! The nurse came in and he told her that this women tried to kill me. Gloria just looked at him. The nurse told him that she would call the police and Derrick told her no, as long as Ms. Thang would leave and never come back, so Gloria left.

# Chapter Three

As Gloria was leaving the hospital, she heard a noise. She made it to her care and she noticed that she had a flat. She called Triple A and was told that someone would be arriving shortly. She said, momma told me that there would be days like this. She popped the trunk to see could she put the spare on. Before she could get the spare out of the trunk, a handsome man let his window down and asked did she need any help and she told him yes. He finished putting her tire on and he asked her was she married, divorced, engaged or shacking. She told him none of the above. He asked her could he take her out to dinner. She told him that she had expensive taste and that he might not make enough money for her. He just looked at her. She then asked him what he did for a living. He told her that he was a High School Principal and he also worked on the weekend as an ER Doctor. Gloria could see so many dollar signs. He told her that she never dated a white guy. He told her that it was the first time for everything. He told her by the way my name is Braxton and she told him her name. They exchanged numbers and she thanked him for changing her tire. She called Triple A to cancel their services.

Braxton and Gloria started dating and she really enjoyed being with him. She asked him what kind of meat he had in his freezer. He knew what she was talking about, he told her that it was a twelve in, big fat tenderloin and it was wrapped very tight. He took her to his mountain home and it was very spacious. They prepared a picnic basked and they walked hand-in- hand until they found the perfect spot. Braxton asked her was she ready to eat and she said let's get it on. He stated kissing her and she started seeing stars. He had very soft lips that reminded her of hubba bubba chewing gum. They had sex four times and Gloria never felt like this before. Braxton and Gloria continued to date. She told him that he was a keeper. Braxton finally told her that he would have to go out of town to a seminar and that he had to do this each year while school was out. She told him that she would be waiting on him to come back and they hugged and made love again without using a condom.

## Chapter Four

Gloria was shopping in Wal-Mart and she was in the television isle. She looked up and she saw this man watching her. She asked him did he like what he saw? He said, I sure do. She told him that she had saw him somewhere before. He told that he was Senator Lewis and the he would like to get to know her better. Gloria jotted down his information. She said to herself, oh, I have to get some of that.

The next day she went to his office. She was dressed to the Nine. There was a female sitting at the desk. When Gloria told her that she was there to see Senator Lewis, the female rolled her eyes at her. The female bussed his office and he came out. He looked at Gloria and started drooling at the mouth. He placed his arm around her and she just strutted into his office. He started kissing and groping her. He looked down at his pants and said, look what you just started. Gloria told him to wait one dam minute? She told him that he did not touch her until she said so. She told him that there was a price for her good shit. He got to stuttering, how, how much! She told him 30,000. He told her that he did not have that kind of money and she told him to ring her when he got. She strutted on out the door. She heard him when he called the secretary in and he told her, you better get on your knees and get this pressure off of me right now! Gloria continued down the hall just laughing. Gloria knew that they were messing around because of the way the secretary rolled her eyes at her.

Gloria was almost at home when her phone rung. She looked at her phone and it was the Senator. He told her that he had the cash. Gloria made a U-turn. She knocked on the door and he opened. He gave her the money. She told him that she had to count it first and then they could get down to business. She put the money in her purse next to her gun. She looked up and she told him to take off all of his clothes and he complied. Gloria told him that they were going to play cowboy and cowgirl. I have to rope you and he said, okay. She roped him and told him that she would not waste her good juices on his little piece of shit. She told him that it was too short and fat like a salmon can. The Senator told her to untie him and she laughed and shut the door. The Security Guard ran into the office to see what he shouting was all about. Gloria wasn't watching where she was going and she ran smack into the Secretary.

The Secretary told her, yes I knew something was up when he made a phone call after, he got finished with me. Gloria told her, you young stupid bitch, I get paid well for my good stuff. I know you did not get paid for putting your mouth on that little dime piece of meat. The Secretary said, you bitch and tried to hit Gloria. Gloria took her purse and hit the Secretary upside the head and she fell to the floor. Gloria said oh shit, I forgot I had the money and gun in my purse. She stooped down to check her pulse and it was strong. Gloria left.

## Chapter Five

Gloria was on her way home and she looked up into her rearview mirror. She saw a man on a motorcycle and he passed on by. She pulled into her driveway and she let the garage door down. She began to put her groceries up and the doorbell rang. She said who and the hell can that be this time of night? She went to the door and behold it was Mr. Rental Cop. He told her that he had been following her for days. He wanted her to do to him what she had done to the doctor, lawyer, principal, judge and the senator. She let him in and she led him into her middle bedroom. She told him to get undress and he did. He was so excited. She took his handcuffs and she cuffed him to the bed. He did have a nice size cock. She put some oil on him and a condom. She began to rub his cock up and down and up and down. He told her oh baby you make me feel so good. He began to scream and he collapsed on the bed. Then Gloria cleaned him up. Mr. Rent-A-Cop told her, oh baby, I never cum like that before and didn't penetrate you with my deadly penis. Gloria slapped his face, pulled his belt off and started whipping his ass. He was screaming so long and he said oh you are into that matrix shit. She continued to whip him until he was just sore all over and he enjoyed it. She finally got tire of him and she place duck-tape over his mouth and tied his feet together. His eyes got big as a saucer and he just knew that he was in trouble.

She told him that you will never stalk me again after I get finished with you. She went outside and she pulled his motorcycle into her garage and let the door down. She keep him bound for two weeks. She tormented him each day that she got home from work. One morning when she was getting Mr. Rent A Cop some breakfast, a special report announced that a cop has been missing and the police department needs to find him. Gloria went into the room and she informed him that the police department was looking for him. She told him that she would let him go and he better not mention her name if he knew what was good for him. Before she let him leave she recorded him on her phone.

The next day she saw the news and Mr. Rent-A-Cop stated that he was blindfolded and kidnapped. The kidnapper did things to him that he would like to be done to him again because that was the best time he ever had and he grinned into the camera. He also said that he was thankful to be alive and he did show all of the old bruises that were healing on his body. His mom was so glad to see him.

## Chapter Six

Gloria, said, thank you GOD, and please forgive me for all of my sins. I am going to stop beating men out of their money. I am a RN and I do not have to do this anymore. She went on line and she checked her account. She had 8,500 in three checking accounts and three banks, 500,000 in a Retirement Account, 80,000 in Savings in three banks and 160,000 in cash in her home safe.

Three days later Braxton called to say that he was back in town and he needed to see her. Gloria told him okay. He came over and he got on his knee, took her left hand, placed a diamond ring on her hand and asked her to marry him and she said yes! Gloria and Braxton decided to invite their friends. As Gloria was being walked down the aisle with her grandfather and she looked on the back row and there sit the judge, doctor, Rent-A-Cop, lawyer and the senator. Each had a huge smile on their faces. She said to herself, dam I didn't know these fools would be her and I hope they do not start nothing, it want be nothing and I want have to do nothing. She finally made it to Braxton and the Preacher read the vows and he pronounced them man and wife. Braxton kissed his bride. He told her that he was the luckiest man in the world.

Braxton and Gloria returned three week later from their honey moon. Gloria got up and Braxton was still asleep and she went to the mailbox. She had letters from each man she had an encounter with. She opened each letter and was threaten that her marriage was headed for divorce Ville if she did not let them have one more shot at that good stuff. Gloria went back into the house and she wonder what she was going to do. Braxton got up and he told her that he had to go back to work. He left and she call each of her blackmailers and told them to meet her at the Omni Hotel because she was going to let them have their way with her. She arrived an hour early in a disguise. She placed some Viagra into a wine bottle for those old sorry dogs. There was a knock on the door. Gloria was dressed in a leather outfit, with a blonde wig, a whip, high hills and black gloves. She told each to take a seat and she was going to entertain them. She gave each a glass and fell it with the wine. She told them to get comfortable. All of them pulled off of their clothes and they just stared clutching their hearts and they fell dead. Gloria had paid for two conjoining rooms. She took off all of her disguise and she left. She made it home in time to have her new husband a nice dinner. They were sitting at the table watching the news and Braxton told her to turn it up. The reporter was reporting that they had found a five people dead and there seem to be no witnesses at this time. Gloria told Braxton that she was sorry for their families.

Three weeks later and there still wasn't any leads. The Chief of Police told the public that they were going to find the killer of killers. The newspaper reported that there were a senator, doctor, lawyer and judge also were found in the Hotel. The cause of death was a heart attack for using too much Viagra and there might not be a killer, the Viagra had to have killed them.

Gloria wasn't worried because no one knew it was as her but Braxton was having a hard time coping because all of the deceased was his friend except for the cop. Gloria did all she could to pamper him. She got up the next morning and she felt dizzy. Braxton asked her was she okay and she said, I hope so. He asked her did she want him to say at home with her, she told him no and she was going to eat something and go to work. She stopped by the drug store and purchased four different pregnancy test. Since she was the DON, she had her own personal bathroom. She took each test, wanted and each one was pink. She was so happy. She finished her job and went home. Braxton asked what she cooked for him and she told him to lift the lid off of the plate. He said what is this? There were four positive pregnancy tests on the platter. He said are we pregnant and she said yes.

Seven months later, Gloria gave birth to a boy and a girl. She name the girl Bailey and the boy Little Braxton Jr. They finally ruled the fives death as a heart attack from the use of too much Viagra. Gloria was so happy and she asked GOD to forgive her. She and Braxton were so happy with their family and they had a great life.

# Women Talking About Adventures of their Sex Lives

Lena is a woman that really loved sex, money and good-looking men. She was talking to Toney Williams for about three years. The sex and money was becoming less and less. Lena started thinking if he's not giving it to me, then he is giving it to someone else. One of her coworkers had been asking her out. He told her that she didn't need Toney's old raggedly dick no more. She could have the light pole that he had anytime she wanted it. Lena thought about it and thought about it. After two months of asking she out Lena decided to go. She called Billy to come over. He came over, he told her he was ready to ride the choo-choo train all night. Lena wanted to see what she was having for desert tonight. Billy cut the light off, Lena cut them back on. This went on until Lena saw what she wanted to see. She said to herself, damn this little shrimp dick. It is just going to make me mad. She finally let the light stay off. Billy slid on a condom.

He got to kissing and rubbing her all over. Lena was still heated. She told Billy ride me, ride me baby like you never rode a pussy before. Billy stopped and looked at Lena. He hit her upside her head. He said, shut up you Bitch. I know you saw my little dick. Don't act like you didn't. Lena got up and told him, yes dammit! You were the one bragging for months about your big ass light pole and I wanted to find out. I am so sorry that I did. You need to get the fuck out of my house if you know what's good for you. Billy looked very defeated as he gathered up all of his belongings and left. He cried all the way home. Lena was very upset with his poor performance. She said, "Lord I know that all men don't have big penises but I don't like it when they brag all the time.

As Lena was straightening out her room, Toney came into the house. He asked her what happened to her face. She told him, she got slapped. He asked her why. She told him because she told this man that was bragging for months about how big his penis was that it was small. I decided to try him out since for months your dick and money been going somewhere else. Toney said did he lick you. Lena said he didn't get a chance because his penis was too small and he was ashamed. Toney said, I can't believe you lied to give my pussy away in my home. Lena said, you have forgotten this is my home and don't fuck with me tonight. I might do something to your absentee ass that you won't like. Toney tried to say that he didn't have any one. He got ready to say something else when there was a knock at the door. He went to open the door. It was the woman whose house he had just left. Toney wanted to crawl in a hole and die. Lena invited her in to sit down. Lena asked her what her name was. She said Paula. Lena said Hi and what I owe the pleasure of this night visit. Paula said Toney told me he didn't have anyone and that he stayed with his mom. Yes I was his mother but not anymore. You can have my little child. Toney called her a liar and said he never hit that.

Lena told Toney she didn't need any drama and to get out and take his tramp with him. Toney begged and begged. Lena response to him was you don't miss your water until your well runs dry. Paula told Toney I will have you if you will have me. Toney just rolled his eyes. Lena told Toney he better take that offer because his raggedly dick ass was leaving there tonight. Lena helped Toney to take his clothe to the car. Toney and Paula went on their way. After several months of Lena not accepting Toney's calls him and Paula got married.

As for Bill he had a penis enlargement and he called Lena back. She told him to come over. He told her I really have a light pole now.

Lena told him to drop his drawers so that she could see and he did. Lena said how great thou are. She put a condom on that pole and she rode it and rode it. Lena told Billy she wasn't going to let anyone else ride that good dick, it was all hers. Billy told her it was just for her eyes only. A few months later Billy and Lena was happily married.

## Jennie's Story

Jennie was an easy lay that really didn't like sex. Her friends told her she just hadn't had the right one. Jennie always told them she was tired of looking for "Mr. Right Dick". One day she was walking through the mall and this smooth talking dude came up to her. Jennie listened. They asked each other others name. He said his name was Peter, she said nice to meet you. He said the feelings was mutual. They exchanged phone numbers.

Jennie and Peter talked on the phone for several months. Peter finally asked could he come over. Jennie agreed to his visit. It happened to be Valentine's Day. He spoke to both of the children. He told her you never told me that you had any children. She asked, is that going to be a problem? Peter said, of course not. He gave her a box of candy in exchange for a kiss on the cheek. He said, is that all that I get. She replied, I don't know you that well and I certainly don't know where your lips have been.

Peter saw and liked Jennie's girls. After six months of dating Jennie decided to give Peter some of her cucu. Peter was excited. Jennie sent the girls to stay at their father's house. Their father didn't want to keep them at first. Then he finally gave in and allowed them to stay. Jennie just knew she was going to have some good meat tonight. They started dancing to some Marvin Gaye, "Let's Get It On". Their clothes started coming off. Jennie told him to hurry up forget foreplay. It had been so long she was like the Energizer Bunny and she was ready to go all night. They made it to the bed and pulled back the covers. They started making out. Jennie instantly realized she had made a mistake. Peter was sweating, grinding and howling like a wolf. Afterward he asked her how did she like it and she said she did. She hated to lie to him.

Peter gave her money and she didn't have to ask. Jennie called her ex mother-in-law and she told her you were right about Peter. He didn't have anything but nuts. They both just laughed. Peter kept calling Jennie and she kept telling him that she just wanted to be alone. He asked her was there another man. She told him no. Peter finally got tired. A year later Jennie saw Peter and another women but they didn't speak. Jennie saw a ring on both fingers. She said to herself, I hope that you are getting more than I got. Jennie finally met the man of her life, his name was Anthony. He knew how to lay the pipe. He made her head hit the head board and her toes curl. All of her friends was so glad that she found the right dick at the right time. Anthony and Jennie got married and he adopted her two girls.

## Teresa Story

Teresa was a woman that loved dick. She didn't care if the man was broke, she just wanted six, sex and more sex. All the guys she had bedded had enormous dicks but none good enough. She started dating Owens, he was 32 years old. He had a body of a 19 year old. She just knew that she could teach him something. Teresa was the type that would fuck anywhere. There was no shame in her game. She was messing with Deon because he had such a big dick, but she knew he had several women. She was mad because she couldn't have the dick when she wanted it. Deon was spreading himself to thin. He just loved his juice. Sometimes he would be gone for a long time. Teresa was getting bored with him.

So one day she told him to get her some brass monkey, the brass monkey made Teresa crazy. She got to riding Deon's dick like she wasn't going to get any more. She told him how good it was. Deon told her to get up. Teresa said NO. Deon tried to push her up, Teresa double clutched him. She had her arm locked on his neck and her legs clutched on his back. Deon tried pushing her off of him for thirty minutes. He finally pushed Teresa off of him. He told her she was a fool, I am not going to ever let you ride me again. He told her she is not going to kill him. Teresa told him to get the hell out. Deon said okay and see you later. The next day Teresa called up Mr. 19 year old and they met on a dark back road. Teresa wanted her pussy ate. Mr. 19 year old told her that he had never did that before.

She told him that she would show him. Before the night was over he was sucking her pussy like a Jolly Rancher. She really didn't want any dick from him but he kept begging. After three weeks she finally climbed on top. Teresa whipped her ass so fast that Mr. 19 year old got up four times. She told him that he need to hold on to this Amtrak train and stay on board. Poor little Mr. 19 year old he just couldn't take it. He told her that she was too much for him. Teresa told him that he needed to grow some more dick and maybe he would stay in. Poor little Mr. 19 just sat there and cried. Teresa didn't feel sorry for him. She went next door to find Miss 18 year old and introduced them. They hit it off good. They started dating and Teresa vowed never to mess with Mr. 19 year old again. She vowed to look before she leaped from that time on. Teresa would never, never date a little dick man again.

## Barbara

Barbara was a young woman with class. She just knew that she could have any man that she wanted. She had tried a few but they just wanted a nice looking woman on their arm. They looked at Barbara as the uppity type of woman. Barbara decided to take a break from dating. The last guy she dated was very handsome and very married. His wife was a young girl and she was sixteen years younger than him. They had a thirteen old son. Barbara and Titus were co-workers and she liked him. He hung out with the top dogs and went to several functions with him. But they never had sex until they got to know each other better. Titus decided to get a hotel room. They took a bath together, kissing and caressing each other as if they was love. Titus ate her out until they were was in the bed and she returned the favor, it was good to Barbara. She couldn't stop from screaming.

They heard a knock at the door and it was the manager. He told them they had to hold it down or they would get put out. They just fell out laughing. Titus fucked her all around the room. Barbara really enjoyed herself. She didn't think about using a condom. In the heat of the moment she just forgot about everything. Titus told her to let him hit it from the back. Barbara knew it was taking too long. She asked him what he was doing, Titus told her he was putting on a condom. He said they were going to have anal sex. Barbara told him I be damn if that's so. God make one dick for one hole not both. Barbara hit Titus with her backhand and he fell out. She told him, you are a very sorry bitch. Her bit his dick so hard she left her teeth marks there. She wrote him a note that said the next time you want to stick your dick in someone's ass you better ask somebody.

For the next few days Titus and Barbara avoided each other, finally one night when everyone had left. Titus waited for her to get into her car, after all he knew her routine. She just had to be cute before she left work. He grabbed her by the arm and told her, "You didn't have to leave me at the hotel passed out". Barbara insisted that he better be glad she didn't kill him. He told her that she didn't have to bite his dick off. His wife was mad at him because it took two weeks before his dick was well and he could take care of her again. Barbara told him to get the hell away from her. He was getting angrier and angrier. She warned him to get back before she knocked him unconscious permanently. Titus moved out of her way.

The next month Barbara's cycle didn't come on. She said it just can't be. She thought to herself, Titus didn't cum in me. Then she thought about what her mom told her. A clown's nut is just as potent as a real one. Barbara said I'm not going to cry. I will hold my head high and have this baby like a woman. As the weeks went by she began to show. Titus asked her if it was his baby. She told him yes and that she would take full responsibility for their child. He didn't have to worry about her child. While Barbara was in the lunchroom, one of her ex's came and set down next to her. He asked her who the daddy was. She told him, it's not yours and to get the fuck out of her face, you pencil dick fucker. He told her I got more dick than I ever had before. Barbara told him he must have grew over night. He told her he was taking pills and it had grown three more inches. Barbara told him congratulations on your new dick and may it get more pussy.

Barbara continued with her cold attitude until one night as she was leaving work and she almost fell. Donald caught her before she fell. She thanked him and apologized for being cruel toward him. He asked her to follow him to the Holiday Inn. She said no but he could follow her home. Donald confessed his feelings for her and that he wanted to be the baby's daddy. She fell back into the couch and said, "After the way I treated you, you still want to be with me". He told her yes and that she nor will the baby have anything to worry about. Donald asked her if they could have sex, it's not like she could get pregnant. She WAS ALREADY PREGNANT. He HAD HEARD THAT WHEN A WOMAN GETS PREGNANT HER PUSSY IS SUPER GOOD AND HOT. DONALD TOLD Barbara HE WOLD SEE IF IT WAS TRUE. Barbara TOLD HIM THAT SHE was to fat and ugly. He told her that he loved every inch of her. He started rubbing her toes. She said oh you have gotten better. Donald told her after all the rejection he had gotten from women he had to learn some good moves to make them happy. He licked her toes. She got hotter and hotter. Donald put his finger inside her and she was on fire. He said that the old saying was true. He put his condom on. Barbara told him that he has more meat than the smoke house. Barbara opened her legs a little wider and Donald dived in. He was giving that hot pussy a work over. He was great with his techniques. He asked Barbara to marry him and she said what the heck, Yes.

Both of them took off from work and went to the courthouse and got married. They didn't tell anyone. Three months later Donald

Jr. was born. Even though Barbara knew that he wasn't the father no one could tell. Titus had finally told his wife and family about Barbara and his baby. They all came by the hospital before they were released Titus family looked at the baby. We can't lie, it is our baby. She asked Barbara was there anything that she could do. Donald and Barbara looked at each other. They told Titus mom that they might need a babysitter when they go on her honeymoon. The whole family agreed. Titus family had not had a baby in their family in a long time. Touts son was a little mad until he viewed the baby. Once he looked at his little brother he said, Yawl he looks just like me. The family told him to calm down before the got put out of the hospital. Barbara had visitation for a long time. She found out that Titus family was very rich. Donald Jr. didn't have anything to worry about and they made him an heir. They didn't get mad about Barbara for naming him Donald Jr.

*Donald and Barbara went on their honeymoon and left the baby with the whole Titus clan. Donald and Barbara made love every night. She prayed and told the LORD, I thank you. Now I know that everything big is not good for you and good to you. Donald told Barbara on the way back home that the Island they honeymooned on, his family owned it. Barbara said, what? He said, I was born into wealth but I never show it. My dad and mom instilled in me the values of life and money. I just wanted a normal life and that is what I have. We all work hard and some days were harder than others. You know the job we work at, we own that too. Barbara said Thank Yo Jesus. He asked her would she stay at home because he had planted other seeds in her. She told him yes if he was pregnant again. She just wanted to take two years off. He told her that it would work. Nine months later Barbara and Donald had triplets. Barbara and Donald, You knew what you were doing that night on our honeymoon when you asked me to stay at home. He knew he had gotten her pregnant because there was a different nut from the rest of them and his family had a history of triplets. Two months after their birth Barbara got her tubes tied because she didn't want another set of triplets to pop up. Barbara didn't have anything to worry about. She knew that her family was going to be taken care of. She loved her two boys and two girls.*

## The Ups and Downs in Life

Jimmy Jones was borne into a rich family. His father owed a lot of land. His mom Shelly had been a whore. When Jimmy met Grace in the honkey tonk fifteen years ago. She was a beautiful light-skinned lady. She had all the curves that a man wanted.

Jimmy drove a 1989 Cadillac Seville. He was the lady's man. All the women wanted old Jimmy. Jimmy didn't have to hit a lick at a snake. Everything was handed to him on a silver platter. He wore the finest clothes and went to the best schools. He was very sweet and handsome but when it came to the ladies he was very weak.

When Jimmy walked in to BeBe's Café and Grill, all of the women stopped what they were doing except for Grace. Grace knew that she was too young and that her momma would kill her if she thought she was looking crossed-eye at a man.

Jimmy walked pass all of those hoochies and he had already had all of them and was looking for something new. Old Betty had gotten so mad because he would not pay her any attention. She hollowed out and told him that he could not ignore her two weeks ago. Jimmy told Betty that her shit had ran it course and there wasn't any help for her old dried out stuff. That her cat had so many miles on it until it could not be overhauled.

Betty got so mad, she threw a beer bottle at him and Grace pushed him out of the way. He told her that she was blind in one eye and could not see out of the other, two-toned black ass, monkey eye dog and with your ashy ass feet, you better be glad that you did not hit me. Because I would not want to knock your black ass into a coma for two years.

Betty could not say anything so she just patted her big behind and when she did that a lot of white power flew into the air. All of the power went on her face and Jimmy asked her was she a ghost? She told him hell now, I just put too much baby power in my drawers. Everyone just fell out laughing at Betty. She could not help but laugh also.

Jimmy thanks Grace for taking care of him. He offered to buy her whatever she wanted. Grace told him that it was okay. Jimmy just did not know it but Grace Mom Shelly was in the back shooting dice. She knew that her mom was up too. Jimmy told Grace to meet him when her mom went to sleep. Jimmy just didn't not know what he was getting into because Grace had been making money off of men since she was fourteen.

Shelly could not hold her liquor. She would get drunk as a skunk and would not wake up for twelve hours. Shelly thought that Grace was getting her money from working at BeBe's but Grace had been selling her tail for years.

Grace made sure that whoever she messed with that she was clean. She took extra care of her body. BeBe's had finally closed and so one had taken old Shelly drunk self-home. Grace know what time it was and Jimmy was waiting in the car for her and she got in. Jimmy turned the radio on and one of Brooke Benton songs was playing. As they were driving, Jimmy asked Grace, how old she was and she said seventeen. He told her that he did not want to get in trouble with the law because she was underage. She told him not to worry because her uncle was the sheriff.

Jimmy really did get scare. Grace told him to just be cool because she knew what she was doing. She asked him how old he was and he told her that he was twenty-two. He asked her was he too old and she told him that he was ripe for picking. Jimmy continued to drive. Grace told him that she really enjoyed having sex in a car and she hated having sex in motels and hotels because she could not do what she wanted to in bed.

Jimmy eyes got big. He told her that he could take her on his property because they had ninety-thousand acres. They passed by three large homes and he stopped in front of the one with the J on it. Jimmy and went into the house and got a blanket and he drove into the woods. Grace told him to let his seat all of the way back. He did not mind. She reached into her bag and got some massaging oil. He tried to raise up but she told him just to relax. Grace started from the top of his head, rubbed his shoulder, chest, stomach and balls. Jimmy had a nice piece of meat. She could not understand why old Betty was upset.

Jimmy was so excited because he knew that he was dealing with a professional. She continued to rub his member up and down. Jimmy could hardly be still. He told her, I need to stick it in! She told him to hold on tiger, I am just getting started. She continued to rub his knees, legs and toes. She started to nibble on his toes and he just wiggled and moaned.

Jimmy just thought that he was going to burst if she did not hurry up and let him stick it in. Grace went up to his chest and just nibbled on both of his nibbles and he just kicked his legs into the air like he was riding a bike. Grace got on top of him and she rode him. Jimmy thought he was hearing thunder and lightning. Grace knew he was getting ready to let go of a mother lode. Grace slide off of him and he asked her what was she doing. She told him that she was ready for him to leg go because they were going all night. Grace got back on and she rode it and rode it. Jimmy was whooping and hollering. Grace said what my name is, he said Gra, Gra, Gra, he could not get her hold name out because it was feeling so dam good.

Jimmy hadn't never ridden like this before and he was really enjoying it. She told Jimmy to get on top of her and he complied. Grace told him to slide that fat back meat into her turnip greens and screw her like he never screwed anyone before. Jimmy put the pedal to the metal. He told her that he was put a dent in to that cat. Jimmy tore that shit up. He was huffing and puffing. Grace told him that he could rock her world anytime and anyplace. He finally let go of his load and told her that her shit was good to the last drop. He just fell on top of Grace like a car that had ran out of gas.

Jimmy told Grace that he would have to just lie there for a few minutes to catch his breath. Grace could feel that fat back meat coming out of her and she felt so good because her turnip greens were satisfied. Jimmy finally rolled over he told her that she had a good old snapping turtle. They finally got dressed and Jimmy told her that he wanted her to himself.

Grace knew that she was whore but a very good one. Her Aunt Sally told her what to do to keep her vagina tight. Jimmy told her that he wanted to see her again. She told him any day that she did not have to work. Jimmy drove Grace home and she kissed him good night and went into the house. She took a shower and peeped in on Shelly and she was dead to the world. She smelled like a whiskey still and had some of her clothes on and some off. Grace just closed the door.

Grace was so used to messing with older men because they did not last long, and they paid her good money not to tell anyone. Jimmy could go all night long. She had to be careful not to fall in love. She went to put the 3,000 that Jimmy had gave her with the 100, 00 that she was saving from messing with the old men. She never set a price because each man would give her what they thought she was worth. Grace heard a thump, so she ran into her mom room and she had fell onto the floor. Grace just threw some covers on her and then she saw a pile of money. She counted it and it was $150.000. Grace thought to herself that her mom was a high roller and she loved to gamble.

Shelly had this thing that she would not wear any drawers when she gambled. She made sure that her stuff was clean. Each time that she gamble she would open her legs and say, twenty dollars I shoot. The men would be so impressed by her not wearing any drawers that she would beat them out of all of their money. Shelly had been doing this so long and those old geezers hadn't caught on. It was like they were hypnotized.

Grace could not sleep, she got to thinking about all of the men that she had slept with and she said to herself that she had been a naughty girl for a long time. She thought about Justin, he was a very green. He never had sex before. She sexed him so good until he started to cry when he burst his first nut. He continued to come around until he became a professional at having sex and he moved onto someone else.

Grace said to herself that she had to stop thinking about all of the penises that she had because majority of them were not good, it was just the money. Grace finally went to sleep and when she woke up she smelled bacon cooking and she knew that meant that it was time to get up for church. She could have stayed at home because she did not hear anything the Rev. was saying because she was daydreaming about Jimmy. She realized that someone was tapping her on her shoulder. It was the Rev. He asked her was she okay? She told him yes but turned around and everyone was gone. She felt so embarrassed. She got up and left the church. Shelly was talking to one of the church members when she got outside.

Grace birthday had finally came and she was 18 years old and she was so excited. She got so many gifts. The phone rang and the person on the other end said what up Mr. Coochie train, you can jump on my Caboose anytime. Grace just smiled. Her mom gave her an evil look and race didn't pay her no mind. Jimmy asked could he come over and she said sure. She hung up the fool and was so excited.

Jimmy drove up in his fancy car and all of the neighbors were just looking. The neighbor recognized him when he got out of the car. Some said, isn't that that rich boy that never worked and had did old fast Grace Hook up with him. Jimmy knocked on the door and Shelly let him in. She looked him up and down and she smiled. She said to herself that grace had picked her a good one this time. Grace came out and then she asked her mom was it okay to go with Jimmy and Shelly told her that it was fine.

Jimmy took Grace to see his mom Pearl. Pearl didn't like Grace because she knew all about them and she thought they were just trash. Grace could tell that Pearl did not like her and she did care. She just played nice since she wasn't on her own territory. Grace and Jimmy sat down to eat but Grace still did not feel welcome. Since meeting Jimmy, she was ready to change her lifestyle. Jimmy's father love women and he didn't not discriminate. So, Grace really looked good to him. Jimmy told his father that he could look but he better not touch Grace or it would be on like a pot of neckbones. Jimmy knew that his dad would lie with a monkey if it let him.

Grace and Jimmy left and went to his home on the property. Jimmy had a beautiful home. He told Grace to make herself comfortable and he fixed her a drink. He asked her about her father and she told him that he never knew him. She told him that her mom was very educated, she worked hard and put herself through school and that Shelly was a lawyer.

They talked and talked. Jimmy told her that he had been to Boarding School and when he finished there he went to England to complete his studies as a Pharmacist. He also told her that he really did not have to work but he enjoyed what he did for a living. Many people think that I am living off of my family. My parents do give me an allowance each month but it goes in the bank. Jimmy turned on the stereo and they listen to Smokey Robinson.

He told Grace that he was so sorry for taking advantage of her the other nice and he had been drinking and his hormones were dancing a gig. Grace told him that wasn't a problem because she really enjoyed herself. He told her that he wanted to take it slow and he wanted to spend more time with her. Grace agreed that they would go slow.

Time went by so fast and Grace was so excited about her prom. She had a beautiful dress and Jimmy was coming to take her to the prom. She got dressed and the doorbell rang. She walked downstairs and opened the door. She let Jimmy in and he was astonished. She told him to pick his lip up off of the floor. They arrived at the Marriot and the music was playing. When they walked in everything just stopped. Many of the students just did not know that Grace could look so wonderful. They just thought of her a trash. Jimmy and Grace danced and they danced. They were the best dancer and the best looking couple at the prom.

Before they knew it, it was time to go home. Jimmy walked Grace to the door, he kissed her goodnight and told her that he would like to take her to the movies the next day. Grace told him that she would love to go and he left. Grace walked into the house and her mom was waiting on her. Grace asked her mom was she okay and she told her that she just had to stay up until she made it in. She told Grace that it was time for her to change her life and to stop drinking.

Shelly told Grace that she had met this Professor when she was gambling. He told her that she looked too good to be doing what she was doing and if it was money that she need, he had plenty of it and didn't mind spending it on her. He also told her that he was ready to get married and he just knew that she was his soulmate.

Mr. Right came to visit Shelly so that he could take her out. He was a good looking older gentleman. Shelly came downstairs and Mr. Right just whistled. He told Shelly that she fix up real good when she get the dirt off of her. Shelly told him, thank you and I am doing it for you because I really do like you and no other man has ever told me that.

Mr. Right took Shelly to a nice restaurant and Mr. Right told Shelly that he had been married before but his wife left him for the mailman. Shelly told him that she was so sorry, he told her not to be, because that was the best thing that could have happened to him. Mr. Right and Shelly continued to date. A few days later Shelly noticed that she hadn't had a cycle in a while. She tried to think when the last time that she had one was but couldn't remember. She made an appoint to see the doctor.

The doctor told her that she was indeed pregnant and almost four months along. Shelly started to cry and the doctor told her he did not know why she was cry because it got good to her and she could not let it go. That did not make her feel any better. Shelly went home and she told Grace that she was almost 4 months pregnant and Grace told her that she was glad and at least this baby will know his or her dad. Shelly told her that she was so sorry but she just did not know who her dad was.

The doorbell rang and it was Jimmy and Jimmy and Grace went out to eat and she told him that her mom was pregnant and she was excited to be having a little sister. Jimmy looked up and he saw his mom and day. They came over to the table and spoke. His dad was glad to see them but his mom wasn't. His mom had a half smile on her face. Grace knew that she did not like her but she wasn't going to let her steal her joy. His mom and dad made their excuses and let. Grace and Jimmy finished their dinner and left.

Jimmy took Grace back to his house and they made mad passionate love for about an hour and a half. Jimmy and Grace took a shower together and Jimmy took her home. It was long before she was fast asleep.

Grace woke up sweating. She had a bad dream that her and her friends were walking in the jungle. Two of her friends decided to take a shortcut through the jungle but she followed the trail. She stumbled upon a crocodile and he started to chase her but she woke up before it got her. Her mom came into her room and she told her about the dream and her mom told her that that dream is about someone not liking her and to be careful. Grace could not think of anyone but Jimmy's mom.

Shelly told Grace that she and Jimmy's mom used to be friends in Grammar School until they got into it. Jimmy's mom tried to fix her up with her old drunk 55 year old uncle and she also accused her of trying to hit on her boyfriend. I could have had him but since we were friends I did not try. That's the reason why she do not like you. Just stay prayed up and Jesus will work it out.

It was time for Grace to graduate, Mr. Right was there with her mom and she was really out there. Several parents were frowning but my mom did not care, she just strutted big belly and all. She was so proud of Grace. Grace got so many scholarships and could go to any college of her choosing. Grace had not made up her mind what she wanted to do. Jimmy took Grace out to eat after graduation.

Grace told Jimmy that she had missed her period. He said pass that by me again. Grace told him again and he said how did that happen?

Grace covered her face and she cried and told him that she was sorry. Jimmy grabbed her hand and told her how sorry he was and that he knew that he was at fault also.

Grace told him that it is so sad that mom and daughter are pregnant. Jimmy told her not to get upset because she was going to be his wife and they would have to break the news to his parents. Jimmy and Grace went to his parents' house to give them the good news. Jimmy told his mom and she just cried and ran out the room. His dad said let her go she can't have her way all of the time and his your time.

Jimmy and Grace decided to tell her mom and Shelly was very happy. So, they decided to have a double wedding. Shelly wore a beautiful maternity dress but she looked beautiful and Grace worn an off white beautiful dress. Jimmy's mom was pleased but she did come to the wedding. Jimmy and Grace went to Jamaica and her mom and new husband went to Gatlinburg, Tennessee. They didn't want to go too far and Shelly was to go into labor. They made sweet love every night.

Shelly and her husband decided to come back early. At three o'clock in the morning, Shelly pushed her husband and told him that it was time. Jeff said, time for more loving, what has gotten into you woman? Shelly told him that it was time for him to take her to the hospital.

Jimmy and Grace were still in Jamaica and they did not want to bother them. Jeff called the doctor and she told them that she would meet them at the hospital. She decided to call Irene her sister and she told them that she would meet them there. Shelly was at the hospital no time before she felt her water break. She was rushed back and Jim flew back there with her. He had to get scrubbed up quickly. He came out to let the family know that they had a beautiful baby girl and mom and daughter were doing well. They named the baby Italy Tate.

Grace and Jimmy made it back home and there was a message on their voicemail letting them know that Shelly and the baby were doing great. Jimmy and Shelly went to the hospital and the baby was so beautiful. Grace told Jimmy to get her a wheelchair and he looked at her so funny. He ran to get it and before she could sit down her water had broken. Grace was only seven months pregnant.

Jimmy called for help and Grace was rush into the Emergency room. Twenty minutes later she had a ten pound baby girl and she name her Shania Nicole Jones. Jimmy's parents finally made it to the hospital. His mom just feel in love with Shania because she had gray eyes just like hers. Two days later they all went home. Shelly and Grace hated that they could not help each other. Shelly's sister and Jim's mother came to help them and Jimmy's mother and father was there to help them.

Shelly ask Dorothy, Jimmy's mom to be the Godmother and she said yes and she was so sorry for all the years that they missed from being friends. Dorothy told her that the reason why she had fallen out with her is because they were first cousins. She was her uncle Clyde's daughter. No one wanted anyone to know but she overhear her uncle and aunt fussing about him have a child by Shelly's mother. Shelly said how, that means that Grace is married to her cousin. Dorothy told her well it's too late now.

Shelly's half-sister found out that she had had a baby. Shelly really did not feel comfortable letting her in but she prayed and she opened the door. Paula told her what a beautiful baby and Shelly told her thank you. Paula stayed in town for two weeks to make sure that Shelly felt comfortable with her. One day she came over and Shelly wasn't feeling well, so she asked Paula would she watch Italy until she get a nap. Paula told her yes. Shelly woke up to the phone ringing and she grabbed the phone and it was Paula. She told Shelly that she had Italy and she wasn't getting her back. She told her that she had had five miscarriages and you already have a daughter so you want miss this one.

Shelly called Jeff, Grace, Jimmy, Dorothy and her husband and her brother Sam to let them know what had happened. They all came over to comfort her. Sam told Shelly that he knew that Paula was up to something when she called to ask how everyone was doing. They put out as ABP on her and put her picture on the news with a twenty-thousand dollar reward. Jeff called up several of his old army buddies and he filled them in on everything and they agreed to help.

Shelly was so frantic, Jeff had to call her doctor so he could give her some medication to calm her down. Grace was so upset because she could not do anything to help her mom. Three weeks a passed by and no one had heard anything.

Paula had made it to Michigan and she saw her neighbor looking out of the window but she continued into her house. Her neighbor knew something was up because Paula was carrying something seems to be a baby in her arms. She knew that Paula couldn't have any children. Mrs. Kelly went over to Paula house and knocked on her door. Paula let her in. Before Mrs. Kelly could ask any questions, Paula told her that her half-sister had died and she was the legal guardian. Mrs. Kelly said, I see and she left. Paula didn't think anything else about Mrs. Kelly, she continues to kiss on Italy.

Mrs. Kelly had a long talk with Mr. Kelly about how nice it was for Paula to take her dead sister's child since she wasn't able to have any. While Mr. Kelly went to the bathroom, Mrs. Kelly was flipping through the channels and there was a news bulletin about a missing baby by the name of "Little Italy," and there was a twenty-thousand dollar reward for anyone who knew anything. She called her husband and she told him what she had seen on TV. He told her to call that 1800# and she did. The officer told her if she was telling the truth there was a twenty-thousand dollar reward for the information. Mrs. Kelly informed him that she knew what she was talking about. The officer told her not to go back over there but they was sending the local authorities.

Mrs. Kelly finally hung up the phone and she told her husband how much money they were going to get and he said, "Thank you Jesus, Thank you LORD, now my baby can get her knees fixed and I can get these bunions off my feet without getting money out of our account to keep our bills afloat while we are off of work.

They heard a knock on the door. It was Paula and she told asked them why they were praising the LORD so much. She told them that their granddaughter had been accepted in an Ivory League School in Japan all expenses paid for six years. Paula told them that that was so great and she left. Mr. and Mrs. Kelly looked at each other and said that was strange. They wonder was she listening outside of their door. So, there was another knock on the door and it was Paula again. She told them that she really needed a babysitter because her boyfriend wanted her to go to a party with him and they told her yes. Paula left all of the needed information with them and she left.

About an hour later, they receive a phone call and it is from Shelly. Shelly asked them was it true and she told them yes and that she was babysitting the precious baby. Shelly told them not to let Paula know that the entire family was on their way to Michigan from Tennessee to get the baby. Shelly hung up and they praised GOD.

Paula stayed out all night long with her boyfriend. She finally made it home around 12:30 am. She called the Kelly's and informed them that she would be over in about three hours to get the baby. Mrs. Kelly told her that, that was find and the baby was asleep anyway. Paula did not pay any attention to the street and if she had she would have noticed the van on the street. About twenty minutes later there was a knock on the door. Paula said, this better be good! She opened the door and the gentleman asked her could he come in. She asked his name and to show some ID. He had an ID with the Gas Company. He told her that someone had reported gas leak and he was just investigating. She told him to look around and she asked him, have anyone every told you how handsome you are in a uniform? He told her too many times to count.

Paula asked him did he want anything to drink, he followed her to the kitchen. Then he asked her where her furnace was and she told him outside. She open the door and she went back inside and when he entered again he had an army with him. She tried to run out the front door but her husband friends were there with guns drawn. They brought her inside and then Shelly came also with Italy. Shelly asked her why she did it.

She told her because she always had it all, a nice home, daughter, a new husband and a new baby. Each man I get and I get pregnant I would always loose the baby and you already had one so you don't need another with your old butt. She told Shelly that she was not sorry for taking her baby because she didn't need another child anyway because she was younger and finer. The FBI Agent asked Shelly did she want to file charges, Shelly told them no, that she just needs some help.

Paula was kicking and spitting, so the FBI call the Crisis Hotline and she was taken away in straight jacket. Shelly and her family were so thankful. They went to say thanks again to the Kelly's and told them that they would send for them in two months to come to Tennessee because they want them to be the child adopted grandparents and they said, yes.

While Paula was in the intuition, she met a doctor and they had sex. She became pregnant with triplets. She called Shelly to tell her that she was so sorry. She was going through PPD and she did not know it. Shelly was so happy for her. She invited Shelly and the family to her wedding and they accepted it but she let the Kelly's keep the baby. Paula did get married and she had triplets. Shelly did not have any more problems out of Paula, she did a 360 turnaround.

Shelly was dreaming again and she woke up sweating. She told Jeff that something was wrong. She checked on Dorothy and Grace and they were okay. Then she got a phone call from the Kelly's and was told that Paula and her husband were killed in a car accident. Shelly was very upset and Mrs. Kelly told her that she needed to come and get the children. She called everyone and they agreed to load up and go back to Michigan.

They had to stay in Michigan for a while because they had to settle Paula's Estate. Shelly was sitting in the Attorney's Office nervous as heck. The Attorney came in and he read the will and Shelly was so shocked. Paula's old house sold for 2.5 million, the house that her and her husband had sold for 19 million, 100 million from the accident because Donald Trump had hit them because he was trying to get his wig after the wind blew it off, 22,000 acre ranch in Nashville, Tn. Shelly said, I did not know she was that loaded. Shelly was thankful, so she quit working at the college and they moved to Nashville. She sold her home and was so happy.

Shelly was sitting on the porch of her Ranch-Style home watching the children play and a car drove up. The man and woman got out of the car and they introduced themselves as the Robinson. They were Paula's in-laws. They told her that they did not approve of their son marrying one of his patients but it' too late now but they needed to see their grandchildren. She picked up one of the triplets and she saw this dark mark on the baby's thigh and she knew that those were their grandbabies. They left a big envelope and they said that they will be back to get them if she did not mind. After the Robinson left, Shelly open the envelope and there was a check for 60 million dollars, stocks and bonds, jewelry and 200,000 acres of land. Shelly just had to sit down and she gave all thanks to the heavenly Father. She said LORD, I am 40 years old with a toddler and three nine month olds. I am just so thankful.

She and Jeff decided to build low-income home on the 80 of the acres in Michigan. They sent for the Kelly's and they were glad to come and they asked them could they say with them and sell their home and they said yes. Each family continued to Praise GOD each and every day.

# Debbie

Debbie was a woman that thought she could never find a man to love her. When she was growing up, he mom always told her that she would never amount to anything. She would never find anyone to marry her because she as sorry, sorry, sorry. Debbie laid in bed and she cried every night. She just thought her as the ugliest person alive. She never really looked into a mirror.

Debbie started giving her sweetness up when she was 18 years old. Mr. Blade lived next door to her and her mom. Debbie mom worked

16 hours days as a nurse. She just knew that Debbie was too ugly for anyone to ever want her.

One night while Debbie's mom was working the 2nd and 3rd shift, Mr. Blade called Debbie to come over. Mr. Blade was 40 years old and his wife had died 4 years ago. He was tired of grieving over her. They didn't have any children.

Debbie locked her door and she placed the key into her pocket. She knocked on Mr. Blade's door and he let her in. Debbie wasn't afraid of him. He was a very nice man. He always smiled as he spoke to her. Mr. Blade asked Debbie was she sexual active and she told him no. She told him that she was saving herself for her husband. He told her that most men do not want something that they may bruise that head on. He told Debbie that he would show her the ropes. Debbie was scared because she had heard stories that it would hurt the first time and it would feel like she was having a baby. Mr. Blade asked her had she washed her goodies and she told him yes.

He told her that he would not hurt her, he started taking off one piece of clothing at a time. He started to kiss her and she was getting all heated up just like she had cooking oil in the pan on the stove. She felt like her entire core was getting ready to erupt like a volcano.

She had been pleasuring herself and looking at flicks on the TV and reading exotic books but nothing compared to this. He told her to lie on the bed and she complied. He was a very good kisser, had the softest hands and she felt like she was in paradise. He told her that she was so pretty. He asked her could he have his way with her and she told him of course. He could do anything except she don't let anyone go in her backdoor. He told her that he was a cat many and the backdoor hold so many "GERMS."

He told her that he was going to eat her out and she told him to go right ahead. She wanted to know what she had been missing. She had organisms out of organisms and she just could not be still. He placed a condom on his long piece of wood. She told him I know you are not going to put all of that in me! He told her to just relax and he would not hurt her. He slide the head in first and she made the awful looking face. He told her that I am a man of my word, I will take it out. She told him to go ahead he took it easy with her and she finally was in rhythm with him. She told him dam! I didn't know sex could be so good. It was a good hurt and he handled her like a kitten. They had sex five times. He told her that he cut tear her draws off of her every night and worker that kitty cat over. She told him that she would be over each night that her mom left for work. She took a shower and left for home and it was 12:30 am.

As soon as she got into the house the phone ranged and it was her mother Angie. Her mom asked her how was she doing and did she have the door and windows locked? She said yes mama you made sure everything was locked before you left. Angie told Debbie goodnight. Debbie went into the bathroom and there was blood in her panties. She said out loud, I really have to wash these before mom come back home. She sprayed bleach in them and the blood instantly disappeared. She washed them, placed them on a rack and hung them in the back of her closet.

Debbie took herself a hot shower. She got into the bed and patted her womanhood because it had a very good meal tonight. I just wonder what is in store for you tonight. Debbie went to sleep and before she knew it her alarm clock was going off at 5:20 am. She made sure that everything was straight before she left for school. Debbie had her own car. Her mom was mad because she had a car but she could do anything about it because her father gave it to her. Her mom was such a bitch, she didn't like her because she looked so much like her father.

She left home to go to school. She didn't deal with a lot of student because many were backstabbers and materialistic. Many of the thought that she was beneath them. Debbie stay focused on her book and was ready to get out of school to attend college. Debbie always went into the bathroom when she got to school but never looked in the mirror that long because she was so scared because her mom always told her that she was so ugly. As she was washing her hands, she just decided to look into the mirror. What she saw in the mirror was such a shock and she just cried and cried. She said, I am not ugly, I am not ugly, and I am so beautiful. She thank GOD for giving her the strength to really, really look at herself. She had pretty brown eyes, a thick head of hair and was brown skinned.

Debbie did have a small scar on the left side of her face since she was three but it really was a beauty mark. She asked her mom what had happen and her mom told her that she fell on a piece of glass. She didn't take her to the doctor but took care of her at home. She didn't want to draw any attention because she was a Head Nurse.

Debbie was still looking into the mirror and the door opened and old Pat came in. She told Debbie to get her ugly ass out of the mirror and I don't was you are looking at because you are still ugly in the inside. Debbie told her that she really felt sorry for her because you are a very dumb bitch. I know you had sex with several of the teacher so that she could get good grades. Now get your dumb ass out of my way. Pat was shocked because she would talk about Debbie and she never said anything. She would just walk away with her head down. Pat just didn't know but Debbie was praying the GOD would let peace be still.

Pat said I know you didn't and she pushed Debbie. Debbie told her now, it is on like a pot of neck bones. I have been trying not to whip you ass but it has been a long time coming and things are about to change. Debbie took her time putting her book bag down and purse. Debbie scratched Pat face up and down so fast and Pat was so shock. Pat looked like Freddie Cougar had gotten a whole of her. Pat looked into the mirror and she just bust out to crying. Debbie told her that she had gotten tire of her and her goonies and she was going to take anymore shit off of the anymore.

Debbie went into the office and told Principal Stratton what had happen. Principal Stratton told her to go to class and it was about time that she put her foot in that bitch ass. She think because her mom and dad have money that she can continue to go around being mean to you. Principal Stratton told her congratulations on her victory. Debbie went to class and about an hour later Principal Stratton told the class that Pat had been in an accident and she would be out of school for two week. Debbie looked at Pats friends and they looked so sad. Debbie turned around and smiled.

Debbie came home and her mom was still in the bed. Debbie went into her room to do her homework. About two hours later her mom knocked on the door and she looked at Debbie for a minute. She told Debbie that she couldn't put her finger on it but she looked so different. Angie asked her had she let anyone get into her treasure chest and she told her mom that she was waiting until she got married. Angie told her, yeah right! I have told you a thousand times that no one would marry you.

Debbie told her mom, you know what I have had enough of your abuse and mistreatment. I cannot help because I look so much like my dad and he never married you. I did not ask to be here, you laid down with him and got pregnant, so grow up. You are not too old to find you a good man and marry. You really need to change your ways because you are such a low down woman and your day is coming. I know one thing, I will get married, he will be rich but I will make sure that I get a very good education first. Angie was so mad, she told Debbie that I know your ugly ass did not say those things about me. I am a good person, then she raised her hand to hit Debbie. Debbie told her if she did she would call 9-11 and she will be charged with domestic violence and would lose her job.

Angie told her oh I change my mind about hitting you. You can hold your breath because I will be dead before anyone would marry you. Debbie told her mom to get out of her room and go wipe some patent's butt because she didn't need her. Debbie told her that she really needed a man because she had a clogged that needed ROTOR ROOTER. Angie finally left and Debbie finally finished her homework. She would be graduating in two months and she would be so happy. She wanted to leave the apartment but her dad own the entire apartment building and if anyone had to leave he always told her that it would be Angie. He only let her stay because Debbie needed somewhere to stay until she gotten out of college. Her father was a very rich man but on one knew he was her father because they had different last name.

Debbie finished her homework, cooked her something to eat. Her mom had finally left to go to work and she was glad. She was so thankful to have a roof over her head and food to eat. Her day always wanted to take her to the mall but she did not want it. She told him to take her to Fred's, Wal-Mart, K-Mart and Goodwill. Angie never knew where they went and she did care as long as she did not have to buy the clothes. Her dad was so proud of her and he told her that when she graduated he was going to go and legally give her his last name. She was the only child and she would get everything that he had. Angie just belittled her every chance that she got.

Debbie got ready for bed and was watching one of her favorite movies and there was a knock on the door. She asked who it was and no one said anything and she asked again. The person continued to knock. Debbie made sure that the alarm was on and she put the numbers in straight down to alert the alarm company. The person continued to knock and she decided to call 9-11 and her father. The person was still knocking when the police and her father arrived. Her father came in and asked her was she okay and she told him yes. The police brought a man and a women into the apartment. They asked Debbie did she know them and she said no. The couple told the police that they were there because Debbie scratched up their daughters face at school and she was suspended for two weeks from school. They came to handle it.

Both policeman looked at each other and one of them said, now say that again and the female repeated herself. The policeman told them to have a seat or they would be locked up. The female told the cops you don't know who I am. I am Judge Williams and no one messes with my family. One of the officers got ready to say something but her dad put his hand up to let them know that he had this. He asked Debbie what happen. After Debbie told him what had happen, he told them that he was very powerful and he could sue her and her daughter for harassment. Judge Williams told him that he did not have much pull as she did because she owned the whole city. Debbie dad told her not to play with him because she did not know what side of the tracks he come from. The cops asked did they want to file charges, Debbie and her father said no. The cops asked the Williams to leave.

Debbie was so glad, she told her dad that she did not know what would have happen if they had of broken into the apartment. Her dad hugged her and told her that he really loved her and not to tell mom. Her dad made sure that everything was locked up and he left.

Two days later, Debbie received a summons to appear in court and she called her father to let him know. Her mom asked her why the cop was at her door and she told her. Her mom did not show any concern and then she told her whatever happens. Debbie just looked at her and shook her head.

Debbie and her dad was in court waiting to be called. The Bailiff told everyone to rise and all did. The Judge told everyone to have a seat and he told the court to come to order. Angie did not show up because she did not want to be in the room with Alex, Debbie father. The Judge called the Williams family up first. He told Mrs. Williams that he knew that she was a Judge but this was his court and today she was a normal citizen. She sad bastard under her breath and she thought that the Judge did not hear her but he did. He told her that since I am a BASTARD, you and your family will spend three days in my jail and then we can talk. Judge Williams told him that he could not do that and he said watch me. Before they left he told the family and by the way, that is my brother's daughter that you brought to my courtroom. I know my job and I was going to be fair. I have heard so much about you and that low-down daughter of your and I see the apple do not fall far from the tree. Her husband finally spoke up and told the Judge please do not lock me up. I am going to grow some balls and when those two get out of jail they will know how to treat others.

The Judge gave the husband his request. Judge Williams told her husband that he better not be at home when she get out if he knows what good for him. He told her that he would not. He also told her that he was going to get a U-Haul and get everything out of the house that belongs to him and take half of the money out of their accounts, cash his stocks in because he did not want no part of that family anymore. She got so mad and kick the bailiff. The Judge added three more days onto her time.

Debbie and her father were so happy. He took her out to eat and shopping. They had such a good time and she did not want to go home. She knew that her mom would be at work when she got home. When she opened the door, her mom was there and she had company. Debbie was shocked. Debbie spoke, the man did but Angie did not. Debbie went into her room so she could study. Her mom knocked on the door and Debbie told her to come in and she did. Her mom asked her could she go stay the night with her dad but Debbie told her no. This is my apartment not yours. If you and your man wants to do the nasty, get a room. Her mom plucked her on her forehead and told her that's why I just hate you. Debbie told her, that it wasn't anything new to her and get out of my room.

Angie went back into the living room and told her date could they go to his apartment and he told her of course. Because I have been wanting to tap that ass for a while. Angie just grinned and told him that she could ride on her train anytime but he have to take it easy because it had been ten years since she had any action on her train. He told her that he would handle her with knit gloves. She told Debbie that she was spending the night and do wait up. Debbie hollered and told her mom date to burst that cat wide-open. Angie shut Debbie's door and they left.

It was 8 pm and she heard a knock on the door and she asked who was it and the person said Mr. Blake. She opened the door and told him hi and why was he knocking on her door. He told her that he just could not get her off of his mind and he thought about her all day at work. Mr. Blade was a doctor and made plenty of money. He also owned his own practice. He grabbed Debbie and he kissed her and asked her could he get some more of that good stuff. She told him that he could have it whenever he wanted it but not here. She told Mr. Blake that she would meet him in a few minutes.

Debbie knocked on Mr. Blade's door and he let her in. She opened up her coat and was in her birthday suit. He asked her could he do the honor and he took her coat off, picked her up and carried her to his bedroom. He laid her on the bed, turned on a little Teddy, and lit some candles. He rubbed her down and she was feeling so good. He had the magic touch. He got some whip cream and strawberries and he place the whip cream first and put the strawberries on top. He ate her and she exploded in his mouth. She asked him could she do him and he said yes. She put whip cream on him member and she ate it off and he was about to burst. She told him to hold on, she got a condom and he flipped her over. He slid his thick, long member inside of her and he slow grinned to Teddy and then he started to swell and then the dam burst. He collapsed on top of Debbie and she told him that he made her feel so wonderful. This is what sex is all about she was all in.

Debbie and Mr. Blade took a shower and they made mad passionate love again. Before she knew it, it was 11:30p. He asked her to stay the night and she told him that she would. She set her alarm on her phone for 5:30 and went to sleep. Before she knew it the alarm was going off. She got up and told Mr. Blade that she had to go and she kissed him and left. He called her to make sure that she made it home safe. She was getting ready to go out the door and her mom came in. She spoke and pushed passed Debbie and slammed her door. Debbie left for school.

Judge Williams had such a bad night locked up in jail. She was in the cell with one of the women that she had locked up. The inmate was so glad to see Judge Williams and she told her that she was going to turn her out and Judge Williams told her over my dead body. The inmate told her oh, you might wish you were dead after I finish with you. She started screaming and several of the inmates told her to stop hollering and spread those legs. Up tight as she was, it would do her some good. Big Shun threw Judge Williams on the lower bunk and took advantage of her. At first she was just screaming no! no! and then she started saying yes! Yes! Yes! She enjoyed those six days and did not want to get out but she knew she had to get back to work. Her daughter did not have it so easy, she got beat up all three nights.

Debbie was glad that it was the weekend. She got up and smelled coffee and bacon. She went into the kitchen and her mom was setting the table for Mr. Blade. She was so shocked but did not say anything. She finally spoke. Angie asked Debbie did she remember Mr. Blade from next door and Debbie said, yes mam. Debbie asked her mom how long they had been talking and she told her off and on for two years and for your information, we never had sex. Angie, told Debbie that Mr. Blade said that he was tired of being alone and asked me to marry him and I said yes. Debbie said congratulations and when is the wedding. Angie told her in two weeks and that they would be going on a Seven Day Cruise. Debbie left her mom and Mr. Blade to finish eating and enjoying their happiness. She said to herself if he did not tell, she would not either. That he could not call or touch her anymore. She was really sad that she not being able to insert his long member in her but she would find another candidate.

Debbie continue to go to school and she felt better and better about herself. She never had any more problems out of Pat and her crew. Debbie graduated two weeks later and receive so many Scholarships. Her mom didn't show up because she and Mr. Blade were on their honeymoon. Her dad and the rest of her family were there. They were so proud of her and they knew that Debbie had put the poor child through hell. Her dad told her that she could come and work with him for the summer until she goes to school in the fall. Debbie was going to a Community College to get a degree in Business Management because on day she would take over her father's business.

Angie and Mr. Blade arrived back home from their honeymoon and she really looked like she was happy. Angie came and got something and moved into Mr. Blade's apartment. One day while her mom was at work, Mr. Blade came over to get the rest of Angie's things. Mr. Blade told her that they must get along and she cannot mention anything to Angie about what they did and she told him not to worry. She could call him dad since he was married to her mom. Debbie told him that that was not happening.

She told him that he could have told her that he was dating her mom. He told her that he could not do that because he had been lusting after her since she was 14 years-old. He just had to wait until she got grown so that he wouldn't go to jail and lose everything that he had built-up. He asked her could he hit it one last time and she told him yes. Debbie asked him to lie down on the floor and close his eyes. She balled her fist up and punched him in his balls. She told him to get his ass up and get out and don't every come back if you know what is good for you. Mr. Anthony Blade forgot Angie's belongings as he crawled back to his apartment.

Two weeks later while Debbie was asleep and she heard someone coming into the apartment. She thought that it was her mom but it was Mr. Blade again. He told Debbie that she had really fucked up now. She asked where her mom was at and he told her that he had given her a sedative. He grabbed her by her hair and he began to take off of her clothes. Debbie fought him until he was too tired to continue. He told her that he was too tried to be playing these game, was she going to let him get some of that sweet tender cat again. Debbie told him hell no! Debbie picked up a bookend and she hit him in the forehead. He had bump on his head that looked like a unicorn. She told him to get the hell out or she would call her father and the police and he left.

After that encounter, Anthony stopped bothering her. He purchase him and Angie a three bedroom home in another city. Debbie was so happy and she did change the locks on the apartment. She began to work for her father and really loved it. There were several guys trying to come on to her. She told them who her father was and they stopped trying. Her dad finally gave her his last name.

One day while Debbie was with a customer, Angie walked in with the glow on her face. She asked Debbie could she have a word with her and Debbie told her to wait until she finish with her customer. Debbie took her mom to the Conference and Angie told her that she was four months pregnant and that she wanted to do better by this child that she did by her. Debbie hugged her mom and told her how happy she was. She finally told Debbie how sorry she was for mistreating her all of those years. Debbie told her that she had forgiven her long ago because she believed in GOD and he is a forgiving GOD.

She told Debbie that she really did not know what love was until she meet Anthony and he showed her how to love. She told Debbie that she was a changed woman. They said their goodbyes and Debbie went back to work.

Debbie continued to go to school and work for her dad. She really enjoyed what she did for a living. One day while she was working and Pat came into her father's Hotel with two guys. She checked in but didn't see Debbie. A few minutes later she saw both guys come down but she did not see Pat. Her mind told her to get the room number and check on Pat. She really didn't want too but went on anyway. She got the key and she opened the door, There was Pat stretched out on the bed, blood was coming from her rectum. She covered her up and then she saw some powdery substance on the bed.

Debbie had taken a healthcare course in high school, so she felt for a pulse and it was very weak. Debbie dialed 9-11 and performed CPR until the Medics came. The Medics took over and told her that she had done a very good job and if she had been 30 minutes late her friend would be gone. Her dad gave her a hug and told her how proud he was of her. He also knew how mean she was too her but she just couldn't let her die on her watch. The Devil tried to stop her but the LORD intervene and Pats live was spared.

Debbie finally got up the nerves to visit Pat in the hospital the hospital. Pat's family were all there. The family thank her so much for saving Pat's life. Debbie spoke to Pat but she was so ashamed for what she had done. Pat finally told Debbie how graceful she was for her saving her life and she did know how to repay her. Pat told her how sorry she was for the way that she treated her. She treated her like that because she was poor but that was an excuse. She just did not know how rich her family was until their day in court. She told Debbie that she didn't dressed the part of being rich. Debbie told her that she was taught what was of value and what wasn't. Things fad but the love in your heart for others doesn't.

Pat told Debbie that she have had a drug problems for year and now her parent have decided to cut her off for two years. First she would have to go to Rehab, go to college and prove to them that she has changed. Pat told her that she was a Trust Fund Baby and she had to do what was right so that she could get her money when she turned thirty.

Pat told her that she was really jealous of her and her thank GOD for giving her another chance. She would have never imaged that Debbie would have saved her life after the years of mistreating her. Debbie told her that she was never scare of her because each time that her and her goonies said something nasty to that she Plea the Blood of Jesus on them all. Pat asked Debbie could they be friends, Debbie told her that she would have to pray hard on that request. Pat told her that she deserved that.

Pat parents came to where Debbie was working and offered her 3 million dollars. Debbie did not want to take it at first but called her father. Her father told her to take it and make sure that it was a Cashier Check.

A few months later, Debbie decided to call her mom. Her mom told her that she was in the hospital and that she had a little brother. Debbie went to the hospital and she just fell in love with her little brother because he was so handsome. The baby name was Little Anthony and the father was so proud. The room was full with each family.

Angie and her little brother was released from the hospital the following day. She asked her dad could she take a week off to help her mom with the baby and her dad told her that it wouldn't be a problem.

He also told her that she would still get pay check. She hugged her father and told him that he was the best father in the world. Debbie help her mom but would not stay the night because she did not want to because around Anthony.

Debbie finally graduated from school with honors and her dad made her the CEO of the company. She asked him why and he told her that he was getting married and Janet was pregnant with twins. He told her about his will, that the bulk of his billions would be given to her, the twins would get 2 million apiece and Janet would get the house and 100, 00 a year for life. He was also giving Angie 10 million just for the heck of it.

As CEO, Debbie did not change, she stayed in the same building but got a bigger apartment and gave her apartment to one of her co-worker who needed a place to stay.

Debbie finally met Donnie who was a Doctor and his family were in the boating business. He was work trillion of dollars. Debbie did not have to worry about anyone trying to beat her out of her money. A year later, Debbie and Donnie had a nice wedding and each signed a prenuptial. He did not want her money but told her that she would still get half of his.

Debbie and Donnie had three children within five years of their marriage. She had a total of six siblings by both parent. They got together a lot. Debbie decided to work three days a week because she wanted to spend more time with her family. Debbie thanked GOD for all her blessing and without him she would not have them.

# Paulette

Paulette was a women that grew up in a home with five brothers and sisters. She was the baby in the family. She was lighter than the rest of her siblings. When she was little her mom broke her back to make sure that Paulette had the finer things. The other siblings she really didn't bother to spend much money on. They had to wear hand me downs. The mom did send all of her children to college. Paul the oldest was a lawyer, Peter a Doctor, Melvin a Teacher, Marvin a Judge, Michael a Fireman, Jane, Clementine, Jessie and Maxine were RN's.

Paulette became a Policewoman. Her mom really hated that but she never let Paulette know it. Paulette talked about all of her siblings and she really did not care about anyone but herself. Paulette was the only sibling that did not have any children. They all lived in nice neighborhoods. Non on her sibling's home would be better that hers.

One day Paulette did a traffic stop. She pulled this young guy over. He was very nervous and she asked him why was he so nervous? He told her that she was such a beautiful woman and he said that he had never seen anyone so pretty. Paulette told him to get his ass out of the car and he complied. She told him to pop his trunk and he did. She search through his trunk and she found money and drugs. She told him that this looks like close to a half of a million dollars. She told him that she would let him go but he would have to bring her one hundred and fifty thousand dollars in a pizza box to her home. If he didn't she had his address and tag number. He told her that he would.

The guy drove off and Paulette said to herself that she really loved her job. To this day she had confiscated over twenty million dollars from dope dealers and no one knew of her scheme. She did not buy a lot, she just bought what she needed. She did have a nice house but would not draw too much attention.

The young man did bring the money by her home and he added fifty more thousands to it. Paulette took the money to her bedroom and placed it in one of her shoebox. She told the young man to pull off all of his clothes and he said for what. She told him to just do it and he did. He did not want to go to jail, so he complied. She asked him had he ever eaten a woman out before and he told her several times. She told him that he better be good or she would kick him in his nuts if he was no good. He told her to lie down and she complied. He started from her toes and she told him did I not tell you to eat my cat! He told her to shut up and let him do his job and she complied. He started again to lick her toes and she started to moan. Then he licked her right leg and then he left. He sled up and then she said, yea though I walk through the valley of the shadows of death I am going to feel this cat of with my tongue and them my medal pipe. He started doing the dam thing and Paulette couldn't hold it in any longer. She was so wet. This young man knew what he was doing. Then she finally slid his thick medal pipe in and he started to grin Ms. Paulette. She started to moan and groan. The young man told her that he was cumming and she told him to cum on. She did and she thought that she felt thunder and lightning when she finishing cumming.

She told him dam that was marvelous. I really needed that. I was really clogged up and you are my Rotor Rutter. I can have a good shot of this shit on a weekly basis. She told him that he had to stop doing what he was doing because she wanted him all to herself. He asked her what she was going to do for him. She told him just giving him her good stuff was all. He told that his package was better than her. He told her that he had money and he did go to college and was a Pharmaceducial Rep. Paulette asked him why he sold drugs. He told her that he had been doing this every since he was about seven. He was just a runner then. He told her that he loved what he did. They decided to take it slow because they didn't know how it would last. He told her please call him Treavor.

All the family decided to get together for X-mas at their mom home. Paulette came to all dressed to the nine's with her eye candy on her arms. She barely spoke but did go and give her mom a big kiss. She introduced everyone to her new boo. She brought a gift for her mom but didn't bother to bring the rest of the family any.

Maxine and the rest of the family just kept their cool because they knew how their sister was. Paulette started to drink and drink. She said, can I please get your attention? I am the best, will always be the best, mom gave me the best and mom told me that she really did not want you all but since you all were her she just raise you all the best that she could. Maxine told her, you know what, we knew mother never cared for us but each night the nine of us prayed to the heavenly Father that he would bless us to get the best education and love our children as much as we could because we did not get it from home.

The rest of the family just shook their head. Maxine told her mom that she created that monster. She told Paulette that she might be pretty in their mother eye sight but she does not have a hard. The LORD loves us all and it does not matter if you or mother does nt. We will continue to pray for the both of you and maybe your hearts will be softer. There were many people who did not love Jesus but he never mistreated them. She told her that the same people that you mistreat may have to help you when you fall on your butt. One day you will fall.

Paulette told the family, I don't need any of you, I just need my mommy and now I have a man. Maxine and the rest of the family didn't get mad because they were used to Paulette. Claudette, told them enough of this shit, let eat and open up the present. After everyone was full, they decided to open up their presents. Claudette thanked everyone for their gifts but went on and on about the diamond earrings that she got from Paulette.

The rest of the family decided to leave but Paulette stayed because she was spending the night. Claudette got up several times doing the night to check on Paulette. Treavor was sleeping in the guest room down the hall. Even though Paulette was her favorite child there would not be any hanky panky under her roof. She did not even call the rest of her children to see had they made it home, she was so focused on Paulette.

While she was getting ready for bed, she heard a voice that said, when it is all said and done and Paulette is gone, who are you going to love the most then. You have nine children and you are not supposed to love one without loving the others. I love all of my children the same. Claudette dismissed that voice and said to go and save someone else's soul because I don't need you at all. Claudette went to sleep without saying her prayers. She got up at 9:30 and fixed a big breakfast for Paulette and her friend. They all finished eating and Paulette and her friend left. Her mom called to make sure that she made it home.

X-mas was over and Paulette was at work. She really loved her job. She was sitting at her desk just thinking about how much her mom loved her more than her siblings. She knew that her mom cheated on the man that she thought was her father. She found out in the fifth grade that he wasn't her father. She was very upset that Daddy Johnny wasn't her dad but he never treated her any different. He loved all of his children. Paulette overheard her mom talking to one of her friends. See Paulette was always was nosey. She was under her mom bed that day. She heard her mom say, you know Paulette is not Johnny's. I just thought that he was going to kill me when he found out she wasn't his. She was too light and had very straight blond hair. The other child were brown skin and looked just like Johnny's side of the family. I just love her so much.

I really thought that Jason loved me. We had such a good time. He didn't have any children by Helen. I just knew that he would be excited when he found out I was pregnant. He just told me to get rid of it because he and Helen were going to wait before they had children. She just had to make sure that Johnny never found out but he did. Claudette was crying so hard, she felt something on her leg and it was little Paulette. She was so shocked, Paulette tried to run and Claudette told her to bring her nosey ass back here. Paulette was so scared. When she got older she told her mom that she didn't hate her she was glad that Jason was her father. He finally acknowledged her.

Helen did not like it at first but she act like Paulette was hers and Paulette stayed over there a lot. Her siblings were not bother that they had different fathers. Paulette looked up and she saw a man standing there and he looked familiar. He told her that he had been standing there for a while and she really had something heavy on her mind. She asked him how he could help him. He told her that he was her brother and that Jason was his father. They got to talking and decided to get together later.

Two days later Jason called Claudette and told her that he really needed to talk to her and Claudette told him sure. Claudette never got over Jason. Jason arrived and Claudette told him to have a seat and he did. He told her that Helen and he had gotten a divorce and she was married again. He did not want to continue to live along. He asked her to marry him and she said yes, yes and yes! The mad plans to get married the next weekend. Claudette called all of her children to let them know when she was getting married and she wanted all of them to attend.

They finally got married. Jason put his home up for sale and moved in with Claudette. Claudette was the happiest she ever been. On their wedding night Claudette was so scared because it was a while since she had been made love too. She could not believe this, she was fifty-seven and Jason was sixty. Jason told her that he would take it slow because they had a life time. He started kissing her and she began to get warmer and warmer. She said, baby I still got it. She pulled off Jason clothes and she told Jason oh, you are still hung like a horse. She told him that she was going to try something new because she never went down on a man and he would be her first. He told her that it was just like licking on a blow pop. She told him that you old ass was going down on me too. He began to do his thing and licked her so good she started to scream. She told him that is why all those young folks love oral sex, oh it's delicious. She decided to ride him and she rode him like a Black Stallion. Then a strong orgasm came over her and she fell out of the bed. He asked her was she okay and she said hell yea. You know what they say if you fall off, just get up and ride it again and again. They both just laugh. They made love all night and didn't get out of the bed until 4pm the next day. She told Jason, that is what I call F-U-C-K-I-N-G.

A week later the family were invited over and they could see the change in Claudette. Jason told them that he knew that he wasn't their father but he would love to be a part of the grandchildren lives. The grandchildren told him that they would call him Big Daddy and Jason was happy. He looked around but didn't see Paulette.

He called Paulette and he asked her what was she up too and she said nothing. He told her that he knew what she was doing and she needed to stop before she is locked up for a long time. He told her that a lot of crooked things were going on in the department and he did not want his daughter to get caught up in it. Paulette started to breathe hard, Jason told her to calm down. He told her that everything was okay and to stop doing what she was doing. Also to find a good man, get married and give me some grandbabies.

Paulette told her father that she was the best and he asked her who told her that and she said my mommy. He told her that Claudette was wrong for misleading her all of those years and that GOD loves us all the same. Money and material things do not make you. You can have all of those things and still be alone. She told him that she didn't know any better. He told her that he would make sure that she learned because Claudette and she were going to start severing the LORD every Sunday from now on.

He told her that I have watch all of your siblings and they are so content with what they have and they shows that they have JESUS in their hearts. Paulette starting crying and no one had ever made it so plain. She told him that she had been so awful to her sisters and she was ready to change and would love to get married one day. He told her that he would not mention to Claudette what she have been doing but Claudette would have to apologize to all of her children.

They did go to church and learned about how the LORD loves them all and he did think no more of one than he thought of the others. Claudette called all of her children together and she apologized to all of her children and she told them that she really loved them. They all hugged and the other siblings told them that the LORD had answered their prayers.

Two days later, Trevor got with Paulette and he got on his knees and asked her to marry him and she told him yes. He told her that he didn't want any shit out of her, he was the man and he would wear the pants and she was going to church each Sunday and she was going to have him two babies. She looked at him and said yes Daddy.

Three weeks later Trevor and Paulette got married. The family was so happy. Jason walked her down the aisle. A few months later, Paulette to the family together and told them the she and Trevor were having a baby. She just did not know but they were having twins. Paulette was in labor, she had the first baby and then the doctor said, I feel something else. Paulette said, I know I don't. She felt another contraction and she did have another baby. She had a little boy and girl. They named the boy Teddy and the girl Shelly. Paulette could not be more happier because GOD had stepped in and changed her live.

www.ingramcontent.com/pod-product-compliance
Ingram Content Group UK Ltd.
Pitfield, Milton Keynes, MK11 3LW, UK
UKHW041603200226
10829UKWH00028B/274